SUMMARY JUDGMENT

"Bleep bleep! Bleep bleep!" The little craft pitched suddenly downward and to the right. The detectors had picked up ranging radar from the U.P. complex and had automatically taken evasive action.

Thomac got control again just over the rooftops, but he noticed an odd blinking, which seemed to come from the floor. It was, in fact, a hole in the floorplate. He bent over and examined the hole carefully. The edges were not jagged nor bent inward. Nor were they fused or melted. The little circle was brilliantly clean.

He looked overhead. Ah, the exit hole.

He shivered, and then began to perspire. Somebody down there didn't want him snooping around . . .

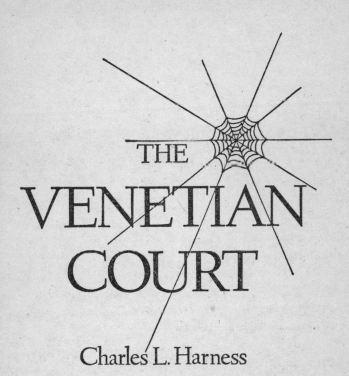

THE
VENETIAN
COURT

Charles L. Harness

A Del Rey Book

BALLANTINE BOOKS • NEW YORK

recant provisions past the mirror room, resolving to find the to-it mirror that hung just inside. The ... could have placed firmly to check his ... face in that mirror. But no more. Later he ...

A Del Rey Book
Published by Ballantine Books

Copyright © 1982 by Charles L. Harness

All rights reserved under International and Pan-American
Copyright Conventions. Published in the United States by
Ballantine Books, a division of Random House, Inc., New
York, and simultaneously in Canada by Random House of
Canada, Limited, Toronto, Canada.

Library of Congress Catalog Card Number: 82-6658

ISBN 0-345-30626-0

Manufactured in the United States of America

First Edition: October 1982

Cover art by Ralph Brillhart

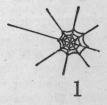

1

THE FILAMENT

Quentin Thomas strode past the music room, resolutely
ignoring the tri-di mirror that hung just inside. Five
years ago he would have paused briefly to check his
appearance in that mirror. But no more. He had lost
confidence in his looks. He wasn't yet forty, but his
hair was already thinning and turning gray. His face
seemed to be built up around indeterminate creases.
Was he already in middle age? He thought his iris im-
plants might need changing again. Or should he go back
to bifocals?

He had to get away, if only overnight. He wanted
to watch the sun come up over the Massanutten Mountains, with mist pouring like a slow river through the
Newmarket Gap. Then, facing the other way, he
could see the cliffs of Stony Man up in the Shenandoah
ridges. Perhaps he could go away this weekend. But
here was this woman, waiting for him in the anteroom.

He walked on past the mirror and its reproaches.
In grudging compromise, he touched his fingers to
his new black lace collar—the current vanity of the

1

profession. Did he really need a woman to review his appearance and/or for other purposes? No. He'd tried that—twice. And they had left him. One, two. He didn't blame them. He would get on a case and then he would become oblivious to everything else. When he was in the midst of litigation, his personal life simply evaporated. There was no room for it.

He remembered.

"Choose, damn you!"

"But I *can't* get away with you—even overnight. I have to be in court tomorrow at ten o'clock. You know that."

"You can't get away, even if that means I'll leave you?" (Incredulously.)

"Don't do this to me. You know I love you."

"Lies . . . lies . . ." Screams . . . screams . . .

She had already packed, of course. And she had drawn out all the money in their joint-access fund. That was the pattern. The first. And the second.

Why was he so good with a female client and so damn useless with a female wife? He didn't know; and he didn't propose to analyze it. And actually he was pretty damn good with any kind of a client!

He walked on down through the hallway. Midway he saw the spider. It dangled from the hall ceiling on a single filament, mute and without motion. He paused and considered the tiny intruder with growing wonder. It shouldn't be there. What prey did it hope to capture within the sterile confines of his apartment-office? It was out of place there.

Or was it?

His entry into the hall created a slight draft, and the silken thread trembled briefly, scattering a slender linear reflection of the ceiling lights.

That filament . . .

The woman in the waiting room wanted to talk to him about a filament.

Coincidence?

He shivered. Were the fates already at work?

As a rational human being, he didn't believe in fate.

Strike that. Your Honor, I misspoke. As a rational human being, I don't *want* to believe in fate. And as a lawyer, I don't *want* to believe that external forces guide my destiny, or that some deus ex machina determines whether my client wins or loses.

But that's the way it seems to happen. I look deep into my subconscious, and I perceive, first of all, that I'm not a completely rational human being. And I see, furthermore, that the free play of my mind searches out fate—which in final definition is simply the logical mix of justice appropriate for all the dramatis personae. That's why they come to me. When nobody else will touch their cases, they come to me. But in the end, it's fate, not me. I just make it happen sooner, quicker, cleaner. I'm the go-between. I make the introductions between client and destiny.

But even as he pondered these oddities, the vertical line disappeared. He peered up and down. Nothing on the ceiling. Or on the hall carpet. His little guest had vanished. He shrugged. But he felt he had been alerted. He would be very careful. He would bear in mind the spider and its filament, and he would listen very attentively to this woman.

He walked into his waiting room. "Please don't get up," he said to Ellen Welles.

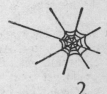

2

JUDGE SPEYER

The screen signal was strident, compelling. Judge Speyer, in a motion at once curious and annoyed, reached across his desk and punched in. The noise stopped and the words of the message jumped onto the screen like scurrying fireflies.

My dear Brother Speyer:

It has come to my attention that proceedings in <u>United States</u> v. <u>Systems</u> Motors have been completed for over two years, but I have not seen your opinion. I wonder how this is coming? I appreciate that you have a crowded docket, but so have we all. We have some interns—third-year students from the University of Maryland—if you need further clerical assistance.

As you know, <u>U.S.</u> v. <u>Systems</u> Motors is an extremely important case, not only for the case law that is sure to come from it but also as casting a light on the economic

future of a considerable segment of industry . . .

There was more.
He waited a moment, then punched the print button. After the record rolled out he ripped it off like a
paper towel. And then he was perplexed. He had read
the message. Why had he printed it? He well knew
what the senior judge wanted. He had known for
months. He wadded up the memo and tossed it into
the macerator. And then he scowled. *Systems Motors*.
He would get to it. Why was the chief so antsy? He
would get to it. Soon. He just needed something to
charge up his psychic batteries. *Then* he could write
that damn antitrust opinion.

Writing a decision was like taking a written examination back in college. Or law school. Especially law
school. And all his life he had done poorly in his
written examinations. Now, the orals were something
else. He did well in oral recitals. But he needed a push
to set anything down in writing. Especially a written
opinion. Another bad thing about these written decisions, the circuit court of appeals could reverse them.
He led the panel of district judges in reversals. Those
dreadful written opinions! Every one was simply a
target for a reversal. He sometimes had the impression
that the appellate panel agreed ahead of time they
were going to reverse him. Well, with *Systems Motors*
he wasn't going to get reversed. He would show them
how alert and profound he was. They would marvel
at the depths of his insights.

For a long moment he thought about *Systems* in
another context. *Systems* could well be The Big One—
the one that would serve as a stepping-stone to one
of the circuit courts of appeals—and from there to
the United States Supreme Court. It wasn't just a
daydream. With a little help from his political friends,
he expected it eventually to become a reality. But not
on his current record. He needed something really

significant. And a big antitruster like *Systems* might well be it.

If he could only get started.

But how to get started?

He needed a death penalty case.

He got out his court calendar and pondered the entries one by one.

The criminal docket offered the usual array: computer embezzlements, extortions, armed robbery, dope, rape, even a couple of manslaughters. But none carried the death penalty. He needed a trial where he could lay the big one on the defendant. Nothing.

How about the civil side? Ridiculous even to think about it. What excitement lay in product liability, class actions, breach of contract, negligence, employment discrimination?

And then his eye fell on the simple one-line entry, *Universal Patents* v. *Welles Engineering Corp. and Ellen Welles*, patent infringement.

This was it.

His heart began to pound.

He could do it. He could wrap up *U.P.* v. *Welles* within two trial days. Today is Monday. Start Friday. Let the poor doomed defendant anguish through the weekend. Wind it up Monday week. Start dictating that damn antitrust opinion that afternoon.

His face lit up in a marvelous smile. Then, as he visualized the final, inevitable scene when the patent trial came to its crushing denouement in his courtroom, he began to chuckle quietly. The chuckles changed to laughter. His pot belly surged like an animal. Finally he got things under control. Shaking his head in deep and utter satisfaction, he wiped the water from his eyes.

"*Systems,*" he murmured, "you and I have a rendezvous next week."

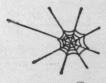

3

WHY ME?

"Why *me*?" Quentin Thomas asked. He studied his visitor thoughtfully. Ellen Welles was pale, thin to the point of emaciation. Sunken eyes accentuated her high cheekbones. He detected faint traces of makeup —as though she had applied powder, rouge, and lipstick, appraised the result as hopeless, and had taken them off again. She wore a dark-gray business suit, with matching light-gray blouse and black tie.

She radiated a strange blend of urgency and remoteness. And perhaps the strangest thing of all: She wasn't using her body in addressing him. Normally a woman's hips, legs, arms, breasts were part of her functional personality. This woman brushed all that aside. Her sole concession to femininity was a faint perfume, an elusive thing that he had to strain to catch, like a whisper. Lilies? Perhaps. Like a single bud clipped, for remembrance, from a funeral wreath.

"Why me?" the lawyer repeated softly.

Ellen Welles twisted her handkerchief in her hands. "My corporation counsel wouldn't take it because it's a patent case and will require highly specialized handling."

"And there are six major law firms here in Port City that handle patent causes. So still I ask, why me?"

"We went to them. They turned us down. But each of them recommended you, Mr. Thomas. You seem to have"—she searched for words—"a certain . . . reputation."

Quentin Thomas almost smiled. "You brought the complaint?"

She pulled it from her attaché case. As she handed it over she looked about the room curiously. "Is this your office?"

"It's an anteroom to my apartment. I work here and I live here."

Why do I join office and abode? he thought. Because it's safer? Was he being paranoid? A little, perhaps. On the other hand, it was a lot easier for an unscrupulous opponent to bug an outside office, search files, even plant a bomb.

"Are you alone here?" she asked. "No partners? No associates?"

"Just me. When I need research, I call on Legal Data. When I want papers typed, I just dictate them to the public steno on the mezzanine. But let's see what we have here." He studied the document briefly. *"Universal Patents, Plaintiff,* versus *Welles Engineering Corp. and Ellen Welles, Defendants.* Standard allegations of ownership of the patent for 'Electrically Conductive Polymer.' Infringement by defendants by making and selling their 'Fiber K,' thereby infringing plaintiff's patent. . . ." He looked over at her. "Do you infringe?"

"Yes. We're literally within the claims of the patent."

"And the patent is valid, so far as you know?"

"So far as we know. All the best references were cited. And it does appear to be an unobvious invention. It seems to meet all the criteria for patentability."

"Can't you simply stop making—what do you call it—Fiber K?"

"The whole corporation is based on Fiber K. We researched it several years ago, got into business, started selling, filed our own patent applications, then Universal Patents issued *their* patent. They were ahead of us. We couldn't believe it at first. They hadn't even done any research. Just a paper patent, cranked out by a computer. A computer-inventor."

"Faust," murmured Quentin Thomas.

"What?"

"Faust. That's the name of the computer. A man named Robert Morrissey invented it. He's in a looney bin somewhere today, but his machine keeps churning out the inventions. Universal Patents administers his estate. Interesting. Hmm." He thought a moment, running through the possibilities. Nothing seemed to emerge. It was hopeless. She was counting on him, as some sort of last resort, but he just couldn't do it. "I'm sorry, Mrs. Welles. I can't help you. I can't take the case."

But she was not to be put off. "Is the greatest defense lawyer this side of the Mississippi afraid of losing a simple patent infringement suit?"

"Mrs. Welles . . ." He toyed glumly with the pen set on his desk and his voice became carefully non-committal. "Some sad things have happened in the patent laws in recent years. Let me give you a bit of history. In the period 1985 to 2000, the United States Supreme Court broke every patent that came before it. In effect, the high court abolished the patent system. There was a strong legislative reaction. In 2002 the Congress enacted new patent statutes, completely removing most of the grounds previously used by the Supreme Court to invalidate a patent. The new patent statute may eventually turn out to be unconstitutional, but until the Supreme Court strikes it down, it's the law of the land."

"I'm aware of all that," Ellen Welles said.

He leaned forward and studied the pale features.

"And did you know that the statute of 2002 makes patent infringement a criminal offense?"

Her sunken eyes glittered back at him. "Yes. Patent infringement is now a capital offense. It carries the death penalty."

The lawyer rose nervously from his chair and began to pace back and forth in front of the woman. Then he turned and faced her. "Mrs. Welles, something is missing here. I'm not getting through to you. If your company loses this suit, someone will die. Your answer to the formal complaint of infringement has to name that person. Otherwise you lose the case by summary judgment, and the court is entitled to designate arbitrarily any person within the management echelons. For example, the president or the chairman of the board."

Mrs. Welles smiled a twisted smile. "I know that, Mr. Thomas. As both president and chairman of the board, I will designate myself."

His eyes rolled up. "Oh, God," he muttered.

She said, "There'll be a jury."

"The judge could take the case away from the jury. He could give a directed verdict." He thought about that. "Who is the judge?"

"Speyer."

Quentin Thomas started slightly.

"You've heard of him, of course?" Ellen Welles said.

"He's known in the circuit as 'Speyer the Spider,'" he said quietly.

"I know. I checked. I hear he's a borderline psychopath."

"You heard right. He's had two patent infringement suits under the new statute. He took the decisions away from the jury in both cases. He gave the death penalty in both. There's no appeal, you know. You must settle, Mrs. Welles. You have no choice."

"We've considered settling. But they want a royalty of fifty percent on the net invoice price of Fiber K. We would lose money on every pound we sold. We'd be bankrupt in three months. No choice, you say? That part is right. We don't have a choice. We have to fight."

"Perhaps you could buy the patent?"

"We tried. Kull and Ordway of Universal Patents told me they would never release Fiber K during their lifetimes."

"I see." He was thoughtful. "And you plan to name yourself as the sacrificial victim—the oblate, as they call it."

"Yes."

He showed his discomfort. "That is not at all necessary, Mrs. Welles. You have a daughter—twelve, thirteen? No reason you should take this risk personally. You can contract with a terminally ill person, someone who has only a few months to live. The laws permit the designation of any willing oblate."

"*I* am terminally ill," she said gravely. "I am the proper oblate. This is my show, all the way."

God, he thought. She's here discussing this forcibly and logically, and she's dying. "I am sorry," he said. "I did not know."

"Lorie's thirteen. I'm trying to leave her something. To live on. For college. If you take the case, you're doing it for her. If you refuse me, I will have to handle it myself, on a *pro se* basis. And I've never been inside a law school, Mr. Thomas."

She waited and studied this man. Ellen Welles was experienced in running her corporation, and she was acquainted with the affairs of the world and with the things that motivated men and women. But the face of Quentin Thomas was a mystery to her. The mouth and eyes were expressive yet, by a curious irony, the man used them only to show empathy with her. The face revealed nothing of the man. He wore a mask. No, not a mask. Armor. Ah, that was different. He had developed this armor as a defense to the mind-gutting requirements of his profession. And she could see now that he was disturbed about the adequacy of his armor. He was probably thinking that if he took her case, the hour would come when his coat of mail would flow away from him like jelly, leaving him exposed and defenseless.

Quentin Thomas was aware of her unspoken appraisal, but he didn't consider it relevant. He was thinking again. There was that patent case on appeal to the Supreme Court—*Universal Patents* v. *Williams*. The defendant, having been awarded the death penalty under the new statute, claimed the statute was unconstitutional because the statute denied appeal. The high court was expected to grant certiorari, but the question was when. Could he persuade Speyer to order a continuance until the Supreme Court ruled in *Williams*? If not, what other possibilities might he hope for? He had heard that the United States Patent Office had now reversed itself on the validity of the Fiber K patent. He could probably get the Commissioner of Patents on the stand, to testify that the patent was invalid. And then there was Jethro Kull, the owner of Universal Patents, the giant holding company that owned the patent. He could subpoena Kull and torture him a little on the witness stand.

And with all this, what did he really have?

Nothing.

Well, he could take comfort in one thing: Defendant's case couldn't possibly get any worse, but plaintiff's might indeed develop weaknesses as the trial progressed. It was like any other struggle involving great enterprises. Fate intervenes and odd things happen.

Fate? The proposition was suddenly beginning to interest him.

She was watching him intently. "Are you going to take the case, Mr. Thomas?"

He held up a hand. "Just a moment, please." He spoke into the communicator on his desk top. "Legal Data."

The response was immediate. "Yes, Mr. Thomas?"

"I'd like the net worth of Welles Engineering Corporation."

"I can give you the public figures, taken from their latest annual report. The charge will be one hundred dollars."

"Can you get something more recent?"

"I can give you confidential data based on the first five months, certain, plus an estimate for June."

"How much?"

"The information will cost you fifty thousand dollars."

"I accept."

"The net worth as of June thirtieth was three million, one hundred thousand dollars, plus or minus ten thousand."

He looked at the woman quizzically. She shrugged. The invisible intercom voice said, "Is that all, Mr. Thomas?"

"Who owns the stock?"

"For five thousand?"

"All right."

"There are three thousand shares outstanding. Two thousand are held by Mrs. Ellen Welles, a widow, and the remainder by her daughter, Lorie Welles."

"Thank you, Legal Data." He punched out.

Ellen Welles said dryly, "I see my internal security could stand an overhaul."

"Don't feel badly. They put things together by computer, mostly from public sources."

"And occasionally by simple bribery?"

"Yes."

"How do they decide what to charge?"

"That's done by computer, too. They weigh the importance to the recipient, time consumed on the data bank, cost of acquiring the raw data in the first place, cost of human liaison in assembling your special answer, and so on."

"So, what's the bottom line, Mr. Thomas? Will you take my case or not?"

"My fee would be high."

"How much?"

"If I win, one third of the outstanding stock in Welles Corporation."

"If you lose?"

"Nothing."

"Who pays running expenses and incidentals?"

"I pay mine, you pay yours."

"It's a deal." Ellen Welles stood up. "My lawyers will draw up the contract. You'll have it in the morning."

But after she had gone, he began to wonder whether he really should have taken the case. Perhaps he had done her a disservice.

In his mind, scenes from a dozen past trials and courtrooms faded in and out. Bitter arguments with judges and opposing counsel. Earnest, sometimes overplayed, pleas to juries. Most of these he had won. But not all. Men had gone to prison because he had not been able to prevent it. Would a better lawyer have saved them? No way to know.

He knew he had a reputation for winning. But he also knew he had lost on occasion, and could lose again.

He knew he had a weird ability to screen his total experience—bring into focus those factors that have a bearing on the case—that might determine the outcome. I look, he thought, at unconnected incidents, and I see a connection. And that connection leads to other associations. And finally I put it all together.

But will it work with Speyer?

That was the big question. Speyer was a crucial unknown. Thomas walked over to the communicator console and punched in.

"Legal Data."

"Here, Mr. Thomas."

"Give me a bio on Rex Speyer, federal district judge."

"One thousand dollars, Mr. Thomas."

"Accepted. Put it on the screen."

It flashed out almost instantly.

*   *   *

Rex Whitney Speyer.
Born 1970. Son of Dale Ramsay Speyer and
Moira Whitney. Father died when subject
an infant. B.S. Biol. Amer. U. 1992. J.D.
Geo. Wash. U. 1995. Asst. D.A. Howard Co.,
Md., 1996-2000. Md. Ct. Ap. 2000-2010. Fed.
judge 2010 to present. Never married. Psy-
chotherapy during college, A. Stein, M.D.
Unresolved Oedipal conflicts may be pre-
judicial to female defendants. Judicial
history: reversals 34% vs. norm. 6.7%. Net
worth est. $4.5 million, Jan. 1, 2021. At
the bench, appears to consider all issues,
but this is illusory. Lacks judicial temperament. Facetious assessment in Alumni
Quarterly, April 2005, fairly applicable:
"Once he makes up his mind, nothing the
witnesses or the lawyers or the jury can
say will change it." Hobby: arachnology.

So perhaps he had a lunatic for a judge. It was
futile to rehash his decision. He *had* taken the case.
The die was cast.

Let lunacy begin.

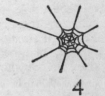

4

A RECONNAISSANCE

Quentin Thomas warily circled the Chameleon far over the cluster of buildings, meanwhile snapping away with broad-spectrum, ultraviolet, and infrared photo selectors. The sign on the belly of his little antigrav read Port City Aerial Surveys, Reasonable Rates, but he did not totally trust the disguise. What was he trying to catch with his camera? He really didn't know. The group of buildings comprising the Universal Patents complex seemed to present nothing unusual. There were three main buildings, two about fifty stories high, the other somewhat higher. Presumably Faust, the inventing computer, was ensconced safely in one of them. Thomas had known that U.P. was multifarious and probably needed a lot of space, but until now he had given no real thought to the size of his opponent, measured in simple physical terms. U.P. was huge. And these structures were merely the American headquarters. There were other clusters in London, Tokyo, Paris, Berlin. The corporate web was worldwide.

He shrugged mentally. Basically, what difference did

it make how big they were? The size and power of the opposition lost the dimensions of reality beyond a certain point. Whether Ellen Welles lost to a midget or to a colossus wouldn't make the poison cup any more palatable.

So why am I in this? Thomas asked himself. She's dead. Anyhow. One way or the other. But because of me, she thinks she's got a chance to save that little company for her daughter. Poor misguided woman. Perhaps I should never have taken the case. But I did take it, and because of that, she sees hope where there isn't any hope. Damn, damn . . .

He broke away from his introspection and looked down.

Below him was the nerve center. Here were the offices that made the main licensing decisions. Somewhere down there probably ten or fifteen floors were set aside for dealing with the patent offices in Washington, Madrid, Pretoria, Peking, New Delhi. And then of course there were the administrative offices, a personnel department, a legal section, and somewhere, perhaps most important of all, a finance department to handle the billions of dollars that poured in.

The executive suite was probably on the top floor of the tallest of the three buildings. He reconstructed the scene in his mind's eye. Ordway makes an appointment to see Kull. The industrial espionage section has reported clear evidence of infringement of the fiber patent. Who's infringing? Welles Engineering. Run by a widow. She refuses to pay, Mr. Kull. Well, sue the bitch, Ordway. Yes, *sir,* Mr. Kull.

And so they had given Ellen Welles the alternatives, bankruptcy or death, and she had chosen. And here he was, circling, thinking, and wondering how he had gotten involved.

There, down the avenue beyond the cluster of buildings—a small flat building, set in the middle of carefully landscaped lawns. What had caught his eye? He looked again. Some sort of flicker on the lawns, evidently reflections of sunlight from something on the ground. Strands of something? He swung the Chameleon over, down the avenue, so that he hovered over the flat building. The illusion of filamentary strands disappeared. Had it been a trick of the sunlight? No, it had been real. He had seen it. And now something was going on down there: Two tractors were moving in adjacent circles around the building. He surmised that they were cleaning up the filamentary detritus. He shook his head. His mind was wandering. What had this to do with *U.P.* v. *Welles Engineering*? He spoke into the recording diary. "It is ten fifty A.M., Tuesday. I'm now at the intersection of"—he studied the flowing panel map —"Kay and Riviera. I'm turning the camera off, and coming in."

"Bleep bleep! Bleep bleep!" The little craft pitched suddenly downward and to the right.

He knew instantly what had happened. The detectors had picked up ranging radar from the U.P. complex and had automatically taken evasive action.

He got control again just over the rooftops. As he skimmed along, he noticed an odd blinking, which seemed to be coming from the floor. It was, in fact, a hole in the floorplate, and the blinking was caused by his passage over alternate light and dark areas of the terrain. He picked up a little altitude, then bent over and examined this very interesting hole more carefully. The edges were not shattered or bent inward. It hadn't been a bullet. Nor did the edges seem to be fused or melted. Not a heat capsule. That little circle was brilliantly clean.

He looked overhead. Ah, there was the exit hole. He shivered and then began to perspire. Somebody down there didn't want him snooping around.

Two holes. Luckily, in the Chameleon, and not in *him*. He thought about that. Two holes in his body. The entering hole, say, in his lower right buttock. The exit hole through his upper left cranium. Everything in between would be nonexistent, totally annihilated. A thin cylinder of absolute vacuum, 0.000 . . . mm. Hg. And then, almost instantly, the surrounding tissues and liquors of his desecrated body would collapse inward on that elongated void, like air rushing in to fill a passing stroke of lightning. Would his dying ears have heard a mushy minuscule thunderclap?

He was deliberately thinking, dreaming up distracting images, trying to remove his reflexive nervous system from his near disaster—so that he would be spared the humiliation of vomiting into the narrow confines of the cabin. But it wasn't working. And no barf-bag— he had never before felt the need. He unbuckled quickly, slid back the window panel, and noted the rush of air. He stopped the Chameleon in midair, its antigravs humming loudly. Quentin Thomas stuck his head out of the window and let go. He felt a moment of guilty regard for the befouled streets of Port City, but it passed quickly. At least he had spared the innocent flanks of the Chameleon. And, after all, he was a taxpayer. He took a deep breath, pulled his head back in, and closed the window.

As he cruised home, he pondered the incident. By whose order had he nearly been killed? Ordway's? Kull's? Probably both. Almost certainly they knew— or soon would know—who had made the overflight. Would they make other attempts, or were they satisfied simply to drive him away? Time would tell. He smiled; meanwhile maybe he'd better requisition a dozen plastic-lined bags from Eddie, the garage attendant. And from now on, he'd have to check the Chameleon routinely for sabotage.

Should he report the shot to the Port City Police Department? What could they do? And what proof would he have that the shot had been fired by Universal Patents?

He laughed grimly. Kull and Ordway were one up on him. Already. And the game hadn't really started yet.

Two holes. What did he have to show for them? Had he seen *anything*? Strands, reflecting filaments?

A close friend had once told him, "Quentin, you look hard, but nothing is there. At first. Then you say, 'It *is* there'—and then by the sacred coif of Lord Coke, there it *is*. You *created* it."

No. I create nothing. I see it because *it is there*. And God knows I stumble and fumble and waste time looking for it, when it was there all the time, staring me in the face, eyeball to eyeball, telling me how stupid I am. And just now I feel very, very stupid.

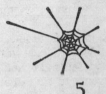

5

WELLES ENGINEERING

"Come on," said Ellen Welles. "I'll take you on our standard plant tour." It was Wednesday morning, and he was there to try to learn something about Fiber K. She picked a couple of hard hats from the rock near her desk and handed him one. "Nothing's going to drop on your head. Just routine."

He shrugged, put on the hat, and followed her out through the back.

A mix of odors hit him. She looked back at him and smiled. "That's mostly solvent. But the sulfur smell is one of the polymer intermediates. It's all harmless." She stopped by a big resin kettle, higher than their heads. "Here's the basic cable reactor. It's a batch operation. The finished polymer is pumped over here to the extruder section." She led him into another area. "Here, we're making centimeter cable."

He watched the finger-thick strand ooze through the die, pass through a coating spray, harden under a strong air stream, and pass to a slowly turning

25

collection drum, where it was rolled up. "What will this be used for?"

"New ocean-floor cable. Better, cheaper, more resilient, longer lasting than copper cable. This particular order is for the Indian government. Nine point five million dollars."

The extruder operator nodded in grave reverence to Ellen Welles as they walked by his station. He stared at Quentin Thomas for a long moment, then with an embarrassed shake of his head began to polish the apparatus frame. Thomas knew what the man was thinking. The workman knew the life of Ellen Welles was at stake and that here was the lawyer who was going to save that life, and the business, and his job.

Poor fools. Let them dream.

They passed on down the room. "Here's weaving and fabrication," explained Ellen Welles. She picked up a window screen from the packaging table. "Plastic screens are nothing new, of course. But screens made with Fiber K offer a new wrinkle. When sunlight strikes them, they convert the photons into electrical energy, and you have a solar battery. With fifteen or twenty screens, you can run your air conditioner in summer."

"I'm impressed," said Quentin Thomas. He followed her through a doorway, across a court, and into another building.

"Delicate things are made here," she explained. "We have to control temperature and humidity very precisely." She took him over to an assembly bench, where they watched women in white masks and gowns work with tiny tools, guided by magnified closed TV circuits. "It's impossible to automate. They're making voice transmitters for telephones, microphones, communicators of all sorts. A spectrum of micron-diameter filaments is stretched between two electropanels. The voice vibrates them, the vibrations create precise electric currents in the fibers, and the currents are amplified and relayed to the customer's transmitter. The set of strands weighs less than an eyelash. The profit margin is quite attractive. The same fiber is used in seismic instruments, in laboratories all over the world. Earth tremors generate microcurrents in the fibers, and these are picked up and analyzed."

She took him through the room and they passed through a double door on the other side. They crossed the inner court once more. "Last stop," she said, as they entered another building. "Another specialty. Spinnerets for space capsules." She pointed to a pumpkin-sized metal globe. "This attaches to the outer wall of a space capsule. On signal, it starts extruding filament. A ten-kilo charge can spin out about forty kilometers of Fiber K."

"What for?" Quentin Thomas asked.

"Combination antenna and solar battery. We have a million-dollar order from NASA."

"I see. What does all this come to, in terms of sales?"

"We expect gross sales of about sixty million this year. If we stay in business."

Yes, if, he thought. "How many people do you have?"

"About one hundred and fifty."

All this will die, he thought gloomily. So brilliant, so marvelous, so futile.

They were in the courtyard again, headed along a pebbled path to the street. The lawyer looked up as they approached a tree with a low-lying limb. That . . . *thing* . . . was it really what it appeared to be?

"Our own special spider web," said Ellen Welles dryly. "One of our people in R and D spun it out of Fiber K."

"But no spider?"

"No spider."

"That would be interesting, wouldn't it?" said Thomas. "If there were a genuine Fiber K spider, I mean."

"Why?"

"That would invalidate the patent. You can't patent a synthetic product that is identical to a natural product."

"That's the law?"

"That's the law. *The Alizarine Case,* U.S. Supreme Court. About a hundred and fifty years ago." He turned and looked back at the web. Several of the strands were reflecting sunlight in jewellike display. It was reminiscent of . . . what? The coincidence was lurking somewhere in the back of his skull, if he could only catch it.

Yesterday . . . where? *Ah!* Long streaks of sunlight, reflecting, shining back at him, on the lawns surrounding that low flat building not far from the Universal Patents complex. But that's all it was, just a coincidence.

"Is something wrong?" Ellen Welles asked.

"No. I was . . ." His mumble died away.

They started off down the path again. The walk curved around the administration building. He noticed a face staring at them through one of the side windows. A young woman? A child? No, something in between: a young girl. Probably the daughter, Lorie. He couldn't bring himself to meet her eyes. She, too, was counting on him. What a pity. How much has the mother explained to the child? What fears now eat at Lorie? What does she suspect? What can she understand about death? She may think of death as a kind of desertion. Abandoned. Poor everybody.

They went on out to the street, where the car waited.

"The limo will take you back to your apartment," Ellen Welles said. She looked drawn, almost haggard.

He nodded. "I'll be in touch." She had probably violated her doctor's orders in giving him this tour. But at least she could get back to bed now.

The vehicle pulled away. One final glance in the rearview mirror. All that—the people, the plant, mother, daughter—done in by a couple of blips in an unfeeling, inventing computer.

When he returned to his apartment-office an interesting message awaited him on his recorder. Daniel

Ordway, Chief Counsel for Universal Patents, craved his company for dinner that evening.

At first, as he crumpled up the tape, he felt a sense of optimistic anticipation. Perhaps Ordway was willing to settle on reasonable terms. Then he frowned. No. That wasn't like Universal Patents. They thought they had a sure thing. He tossed the wad into the waste-basket. It would be something else. He had grim forebodings.

Should he carry a weapon?

The thought made him smile.

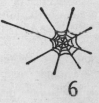

6

ORDWAY'S OFFER

Daniel Ordway sipped at his cup of after-dinner coffee. "You have an impressive track record, Mr. Thomas."

"I've won my share." Here it comes, he thought.

"U.P. needs a, ah, litigation chief."

Well, there it is, finally, out in the open. Like hell U.P. needs a litigation chief. Ordway has instructions to buy me. Kull has put him up to this. Quentin Thomas could even reconstruct the Kull-Ordway conversation that led to that moment.

Kull: It's insurance, Ordway. Get him off the case.

Ordway: He's good but he's not that good. He can't, ah, hurt us. I can handle Speyer.

Kull: Get him off, Ordway.

Ordway: Yes, Mr. Kull.

Quentin Thomas was inclined to agree with Ordway. He couldn't hurt U.P., and it was quite unnecessary to buy him. On the other hand, the confrontation was flattering. *That,* he liked.

Ordway looked at him expectantly, already certain what the answer would be. The U.P. attorney was actually a decent-looking chap. Gray-flecked hair, carefully tonsured. His smooth pink cheeks, closely shaved and delicately perfumed, might have been those of an apprentice lawyer freshly joining the U.P. legal group. Yet he must be about my age, Thomas mused. How can a man with murder in his heart look so innocent? And then he caught it: a thing about the eyes. The mouth smiled, but not the eyes. The eyes were cold steel, and there were no laugh lines at the edges.

Thomas temporized. "Litigation chief, Ordway? I thought that was *your* function."

"It is, ah, for now. But Mr. Kull wants to move me up to head the international licensing operation."

"Are you offering me a job, Mr. Ordway?"

"One million a year, with stock options and sundry other fringe benefits."

It was a fabulous offer, and Quentin Thomas realized that his jaw was supposed to drop in stunned disbelief. Actually, he didn't feel anything. "You realize," he observed mildly, "Welles Engineering has just retained me."

Ordway shrugged. "Let us be realistic, Mr. Thomas."

"I'd like that."

"Then stop and think a moment. You can't possibly win. The smart thing for you to do is to withdraw and come over to our side."

Quentin Thomas took a sip of coffee. His eyes met Ordway's briefly. If only the bastard didn't look so superficially decent! It suddenly occurred to him that if he and Ordway were put into a police line-up, and ten victims were asked to pick out the embezzler or the drug addict or the purse snatcher, he, Thomas, would be fingered, and Ordway would go free. "Why," he asked, "do you think you're going to win?"

"Speyer's our trial judge."

"I know that."

"Speyer the, ah, Spider. A hanging judge, to descend to the vernacular."

"Quite so," Thomas agreed. "But then there's *U.P.* v. *Williams*. The high court will certainly grant certiorari. In my humble opinion they're going to decide the patent statute is unconstitutional. We're moving for a continuance the first thing Friday morning."

Ordway smiled faintly. "You won't get it, Mr. Thomas. And even if you do, it won't help you, because the Supreme Court is going to rule that the patent statute, death penalty and all, is indeed constitutional."

Ordway was predicting a five–four decision favorable to Universal Patents. Had U.P. bought themselves five Supreme Court justices? No. Quentin Thomas couldn't bring himself even to imagine it.

"I see," Thomas said. His voice was grave, measured. "With all that going for you, why do you need me?"

"Insurance, Thomas."

"And you're leaving it up to me to figure a graceful way to abandon Ellen Welles?"

"You'll, ah, think of something." Ordway's lip curled.

Quentin Thomas could see the workings of the man's mind. The bribe was striking home; already Ordway was feeling contempt for him. "Your offer is a little on the low side," said Thomas.

"A little low? Well, what did you have in mind?"

"Fifty-one percent of the outstanding common stock entitled to vote for the election of directors. More coffee, Ordway?"

His adversary gave him a puzzled half smile. "I, ah, I don't think I heard—"

"You heard. Fifty-one percent."

Ordway was evidently having trouble with this final devolution, this impossible nonacceptance. Thomas watched the man's face almost in sympathy. One instant Ordway seemed to understand, but in the very next instant he seemed not to understand. It was like watching the ball on a roulette wheel fall into red, then into black, then into red. Where would it conclude?

Then Ordway seemed to get it all together. His face coalesced and the smooth pink cheeks grew hard. "I see," he said. "You want control of the corporation."

"Yes."

"With, ah, control you could drop this case against Welles."

"Inter alia. Among other things."

"I think this leaves us at an impasse, Mr. Thomas. I must now report failure to Mr. Kull. His, ah, reaction . . ." His voice trailed off.

Quentin Thomas helped him finish. "He will be disappointed."

"Yes, of course."

"But we're still willing to settle," said Thomas. "Give us a nonexclusive license at a reasonable royalty. Ask Kull to release Fiber K to us, Ordway. That's all we want."

Ordway's stomach brushed against the table as he struggled to get up. His coffee cup fell over, and he was barely able to rescue his chair. "We will never release that fiber. We'll hold on to that as long as we live, and, ah, maybe longer." He turned and strode out.

Quentin Thomas watched the departure thoughtfully. Would Kull now try to kill him? Again? Would he have to start carrying a gun? He sighed. He couldn't handle this litigation while looking over his shoulder. Still, there were certain minimal precautions to be taken.

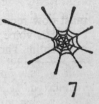

7

AT THE PIANO

Quentin Thomas had long held the theory that music —certain kinds of music, that is—had the power to alter the chemistry of the cerebral cells, actually to synthesize molecules of neomorphine that would send messages to relax his sympathetic nervous system. Music, he felt, did different things for different people. Einstein loved the violin. And how about Cellini, on the flute, and those marvelous golden castings? And even the politicians got into the act: witness Harry Truman at the piano. Sometimes Thomas wondered if his theory also worked in reverse. Had the great Beethoven relaxed with a few choice differential equations while composing the *Eroica*? Had Schubert hummed idly through Euclid on the way to not finishing his great B-Minor Symphony? Somehow Quentin Thomas doubted it. They were probably all numbers-blind. Richard Wagner couldn't add two and two, and his mistress Cosima had to balance the checkbook and keep the household accounts. Chopin left his financial affairs to George Sand.

Thomas sat at the Steinway and started with a Chopin nocturne, the B-Flat Minor, Opus 9. Then that gentle, idyllic bit from the great Pole's *Les Sylphides*.

With a measure of chagrin, he noticed that though his body was relaxing, his mind was still concentrating on *U.P.* v. *Welles*. And what was more, somewhere down in the deepest folds of his cerebral cortex, in an area untouched by the anodynes of Frederic Chopin, an idea was trying to wriggle out into his open mind. His hands fell to his sides and he stared for a long while at the open music book. But nothing tangible crystallized. It was like staring at a black dot on a white background: After a time the dot simply disappeared.

He stifled a groan and rose to his feet. At the doorway, just before he turned off the light, he looked back. Something about the nocturne had not been quite right. Wrong composer? . . . His subconscious mind was trying to tell him something, and he was too dense to get the message.

Intrigued and slightly annoyed, he returned to the piano and looked at the cover of the Chopin book. It was an old edition, a reprint of an arrangement by Klindworth, one of the great music critics of the nineteenth century. Klindworth—that was it. Klindworth was the starting point for whatever his subconscious was telling him. From Klindworth his mind would lead him to the next—what? Another composer? Beethoven? He let his mind relax. Who? Who? Tchaikovsky?

Dead end. Block. He was trying too hard. Klindworth . . . Tchaikovsky. He shrugged. The association meant nothing to him. How could a music critic and a Russian composer save the life of Ellen Welles?

He turned off the light and shuffled back to bed.

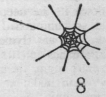

8

SOME HISTORY

Quentin Thomas pulled down a little volume from his library shelves. It opened almost automatically at the right place. He had, of course, been there before. Many times.

He closed the pages thoughtfully. This legislation with its notorious Section 455—the death penalty— had originated in the Senate, cleared Senate hearings, been rubber-stamped by the Conference Committee, passed the House, and had been signed the next day by the President.

Hadn't anybody read it? Hadn't anyone taken note of Section 455?

Even more puzzling, how had that catastrophic 455 gotten into the draft bill in the first place? Granted that the patent system had hit bottom by the year 2000, wasn't the death penalty for infringers a little drastic? Who had asked for it? Had there been a public outcry at the time? He couldn't remember.

He replaced the statute book, walked into his computer room, sat at the console, and punched in. "Give the original text of the new Patent Statute, the very first draft."

Page 1 jumped onto his screen.

Senate Bill 3233
106th Congress
Offered by Mr. Wilford Berwin on
February 20, 2002
To revise the Patent Laws.
AN ACT
To restore the patent system of the United States; to encourage industrial innovation; to protect . . .

He flash-read the whole statute. No Section 455. In fact, nothing at all in it about the death penalty. Curious.

"Give me the House version," he said.

Page 1 appeared on his screen. He quickly scanned the entire bill. Save for the heading it was almost identical to the Senate version. No death penalty. Sometime, somewhere, somebody had sneaked it in.

"Show me the first version containing Section 455."

The screen lit up again.

Senate Bill 3233
106th Congress
Offered by Mr. Wilford Berwin on
April 3, 2002

He scrolled down to Section 455. Well, there it was. The wolf among the lambs. Who had let it into the fold?

He asked the computer: "Did the Senate Patent Subcommittee hold a hearing on this bill?"

"The Senate Patent Subcommittee held a hearing on April 15, 2002, Mr. Wilford Berwin, Chairman."

"Who testified?"

"Two witnesses. Mr. Jethro Kull, of Universal Patents, and his lawyer, Mr. Daniel Ordway."

Aha! We're getting warm. "Give me the hearing, in holo." He switched on the 3-D panoramic stage.

The scene showed an ordinary Senate hearing room. Senator Berwin and his one-man staff were tiny figures at the head of the big table. The room was almost empty. The two witnesses, and two industry representatives. No reporters. Who could get excited about a revision to the patent laws?

In the diminutive drama Senator Berwin banged his gavel and formally opened the hearing. After studying his notes, the senator said, "We will hear first from Mr. Jethro Kull. Will you come forward, Mr. Kull, and be sworn in?"

The miniature Jethro Kull stepped up to the witness chair and was duly sworn.

"Do you have a statement, Mr. Kull?" Senator Berwin asked.

"I do, Mr. Chairman. And with the committee's permission, I'd like to read it into the record."

"Proceed, Mr. Kull."

"Thank you, Mr. Chairman. I am president and technical director of Universal Patents, a new, small, and struggling organization. We invent for a living. Our stock-in-trade is new and useful inventions, which we license to industry. Industry can profit from our program, and so can we. However, if we are to continue to exist, we must have a strong patent statute. The courts have got to stop invalidating every patent that comes before them. Patent infringers are basically thieves, and they should be punished as thieves."

After Kull finished, Ordway came to the stand. He elaborated on Kull's theme. "Already, our copyright laws make it a criminal offense to pirate musical tapes and movie tapes. In Brazil, it is a prison offense to infringe a patent. We need at least an equal deterrent for patent infringement in this country."

"Do you have any specific deterrent in mind, Mr. Ordway?" Senator Berwin asked.

Quentin Thomas stopped the tape right there, freezing the little tableau. He focused on the senator's eyes. Then he magnified to life size. The pupils of Senator Berwin's eyes were definitely dilated. The lawyer studied the dark pupillary discs for a moment. He needed to see the retinal capillaries. They would show the pulse beat, and he was almost certain they were throbbing away at a tremendous rate. He doubled the magnification once more, tuned in the infrared scanner, and started the tape again. And there they were: a living, vital, filamentary web, shining out of the ocular darkness, surging with every heartbeat. And fast, very fast.

"Retain the record for the polygraph," he ordered.

"Retained," the computer acknowledged.

He ran the tape backward to catch the question again. This time he plugged in the voice-stress analyzer and respiration counter. He listened to the senator's words carefully once more, and watched the polygraph side bands on the screen.

`Pulse,` per retinal capillaries: 124— compared with 70, normal.
`Respiration:` The senator was breathing at 64 per minute—four times normal.
`Voice stress:` Right off the graph.

The senator was extremely agitated about something.

Quentin Thomas let the scenario proceed in slow motion. Lawyer Ordway answered the senator's query. "Do I have a specific deterrent in mind? Well, Mr. Chairman, yes, I do. A mere slap on the wrist won't work. Not even a substantial fine. We need something really, ah, effective, something that people will pay attention to. I suggest the, ah, death penalty. With no appeal."

And there it was. Quentin Thomas stopped the motion and replayed Ordway's answer for the polygraph. He couldn't catch the man's eyes to get a pulse rate, but the voice stress and respiration were clearly supernormal.

Kull and Ordway and Berwin. Those conniving bastards.

He rolled the tape again.

The senator was speaking. "Would the death penalty be constitutional, Mr. Ordway?"

"In my opinion, Mr. Chairman, it would violate no, ah, provision of the constitution."

"Due process doesn't trouble you?"

They even made a game of it, Quentin Thomas thought grimly.

"Certainly not, Mr. Chairman."

And shortly after that the hearing concluded.

And thus was murder sanctified.

He punched out.

But why had Berwin gone along with it?

He punched in to his financial service. "Show all ownership of outstanding Universal Patents voting stock," he commanded.

The answer flashed back instantly. "Robert Morrissey, two thousand shares. One thousand shares by U.P. Voters, Inc."

"Give me ownership of U.P. Voters, Inc."

"Data unavailable."

He wasn't surprised. He punched in again. "Legal Data."

"Here, Mr. Thomas."

"I'd like ownership of U.P. Voters, Inc."

"Five thousand dollars."

"Accepted."

"Total shares outstanding, one thousand. Jethro

Kull, 501; Daniel Ordway, 250; W-slash-B Trust Fund, 249."

And who, he thought to himself, is the beneficiary of the W/B Trust Fund? With grim foreknowledge, he knew.

But he wanted to have it stated. "Who," he asked, "is the beneficiary of the W/B Trust Fund?"

"Five thousand dollars."

"Accepted."

"The beneficiary is former senator Wilford Berwin."

The lawyer felt his throat begin to fill. He coughed, then he said, "Thank you."

"Always a pleasure, Mr. Thomas."

So Kull had bought the former subcommittee chairman, and the death penalty had been smuggled in. Nobody had picked it up. The joint House and Senate revision committee had missed it. The full House and the full Senate had voted the bill in, apparently without reading it.

But that was just the tip of the iceberg. Ex-Senator Wilford Berwin was now Chief Justice of the United States Supreme Court.

Quentin Thomas wondered at his lack of reaction. He felt no shock, no dismay. What should he feel? If anything, he felt only a vague sense of betrayal. The man who stood at the pinnacle of his profession, the one man who should serve as a moral and professional example for every lawyer in the country, had been bought.

In time the facts could be flushed out. Berwin would resign and would probably be indicted. But all that lay weeks into the future. Meanwhile, the high court would decide whether to grant certiorari in *U.P.* v. *Williams*. He thought about that. Williams was appealing the death sentence rendered by the federal trial court. The circuit court of appeals had refused to take the appeal, so it had gone straight to the Supreme Court. The nine Supreme Court justices would have to vote on the question of whether they would take the case. If four justices voted yea, the high court would grant certiorari and would hear the final appeal. Berwin, of course, would vote against certiorari. But for his vote to be effective he would have to persuade five additional justices to vote along with him. Thomas doubted that the chief justice could do that. So the Supreme Court would probably take the case. And *then* what? Berwin, to earn his blood money, would next have to rule against Williams on the final decision vote. And here again he would need support. Could the old fraud produce a five–four decision affirming Williams's death sentence? Quentin Thomas thought back to Ordway's prediction at the close of their abortive dinner: The high court will find the statute constitutional. In his mind, Quentin Thomas ticked off the names. First— Frankland, Collane, Oberdorf, the three conservatives who always voted with Berwin. Could the chief justice break out one more? Not Heinman—he was known to be against the death penalty in principle. Nor Buford, nor Lenoir, the arch liberals. Nor Cushing, the former Baptist minister. That left Martin, newly appointed from the Circuit Court of Appeals for the Ninth Circuit. Difficult to appraise the Californian. No pattern in his few appellate decisions. Martin would be the pivot on which the case turned. Kull and Ordway had probably already surmised this. Had they tried to buy Martin?

There was precedent for corrupting a judge. Quentin Thomas smiled grimly as he looked up at a fair-sized photochrome portrait hanging on the facing wall. Sir Francis Bacon, Learned Counsel to Elizabeth I, Lord Chancellor to James I. The highest judge in the realm.

Quentin Thomas had bought the creation in his first year out of law school. He had been cynical then; now he was just tired. At the bottom of the portrait were several lines in Gothic lettering, too small to read from afar. No matter. He had memorized the passage long ago.

Judges ought to be more learned than witty, more reserved than plausible, more advised than con-

fident. Above all things, integrity is their portion
and proper virtue. The courtroom is a hallowed
place, where not only the footpace and precincts
ought to be preserved without scandal and cor-
ruption.

In 1621, at his zenith, Sir Francis had been con-
victed of selling his decisions. Prices per case ran
from £50 to £2000, plus gifts of clothes and jewelry.
Nor did he discriminate: He took from both sides. The
king pardoned him, thus cutting short an indefinite
term in the Tower.

The picture had been cleverly constructed. Examined
in a certain way, the handsome studious face seemed to
lift in a half smile and the right eye to wink. Quentin
Thomas grinned back—but wolfishly, and without
humor. You had a little bad luck, Sir Francis. Not to
worry. You have Berwin and Speyer to carry your
torch. Hard to know which is worse. No, actually it's
easy. With Berwin it's merely a question of money,
but Speyer uses his high office to satisfy his blood
lusts.

He closed down the computer, turned out the lights,
and left the room.

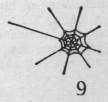

9

KIRK ALLOWAY

On the night before the trial, Quentin Thomas slipped into the side door of the chapel of Kirk Alloway. The room was dark and empty. The altar, a blend of Christian, Jewish, and agnostic themes, offered the only light. Anyone could come in here to think, to worship, to plan weekend activities, or just to doze off for half an hour.

Why was he there? He didn't know. He had been passing by, and the impulse had struck him. But why had he been passing by? Well, face it. He had come deliberately, to straighten his thinking about Ellen Welles. Her trial starts tomorrow, Friday. Then we have Saturday and Sunday to thrash around in, looking for more arguments and defenses. Monday, she dies. Unless I can come up with something.

He walked back to the rear pew and sat down. He heard a noise, forward and to his right. The side door was opening. He watched curiously from the anonymity of semidarkness. A woman entered, veiled, slightly stooped, as though carrying an intolerable burden. She stood in the little entranceway, apparently undecided what to do next.

He recognized her. Ellen Welles. In a moment her eyes would adjust to the gloom, and she would turn, look the room over, and see him. That would not be right. Tomorrow her trauma would begin; until then she was entitled to her privacy.

How to get out? He looked about the rear areas. No exits. The rear wall was lined with little consultation booths, all with open doors. Soundlessly and with head down he scurried into the center booth. The door whisked shut behind him and a little overhead light came on.

The console screen was flashing, "Please sit down." He sat.

"You will find a cranial cap on the ledge to your right," read the screen. "It is perfectly sanitary. Please put it on."

Intrigued, the lawyer found the cap and set it carefully on his head.

"Good," said a voice within his skull. "Now we can talk. What goes on here is strictly private. This booth is completely soundproofed. To start, please state your name."

Quentin Thomas hesitated. He wasn't really there to consult a consolation computer. He simply wished to avoid disturbing Ellen Welles, who, for all he knew, was in a like booth at that very moment, listening to an identical question, and answering it honestly. What would the computer do for her?

"Your name, please?" the voice within his head repeated.

"Ellen Welles," he said.

"Sex?"

Was the machine going to let him get away with this masquerade? "Female."

"Age?"

"Thirty-four."

"Married?"

"Widowed."

"Oh, I'm sorry, Mrs. Welles. Children?"

"One girl, thirteen, Lorie."

"Mrs. Welles, are you here because something is troubling you?"

"Yes."

"Now, Mrs. Welles, I'm going to show you a list of things on the screen. Study this listing carefully."

Quentin Thomas watched the outlines form on the glazed surface.

1. Money
2. Job
3. Family, relatives, friends
4. Sex life
5. Sickness
6. . . .

The list scrolled on and on.

"Which one of these areas seems to offer you the most difficulty, Mrs. Welles?"

"Sickness," Quentin Thomas said. "Then family."

"Are you ill, Mrs. Thomas?"

"Yes."

"Do you have a terminal illness?"

"Yes."

"How long do you have?"

The lawyer had to think a moment. He said, "I may die on Monday next."

"Have you provided for Lorie?"

"To the best of my ability."

"I should point out to you, Mrs. Welles, certain services offered by Kirk Alloway. We can provide a complete funeral, with burial plot, graveside service, and so on. A schedule of prices is available in our front office, nine thirty to five on weekdays. And you may wish to set up a trust fund for Lorie. Our finance officer would be glad to review this with you, same hours."

"No," Quentin Thomas said.

"Now then, Mrs. Welles, look at the screen again, if you please."

The lines flashed out:

A. I wish to review the high points of my life.

B. I wish to construct penitential sequences concerning injuries I have done others during my life.

C. I would like to know more about what will happen to me after I die.

"Do you see anything there that interests you, Mrs. Welles?"

"The last one," Quentin Thomas said.

"You have selected the most difficult one of the three. To facilitate communication on this subject, we would recommend that you light incense."

"Incense? How?"

A small brass tripod unfolded from the wall before him.

"Press the blue button beside the tripod," the voice said.

He did. A thumb-sized fibrous cube dropped from a slot in the wall.

"Your incense, Mrs. Welles. Just drop it in the bowl of the tripod."

Shades of the Delphic oracle! Quentin Thomas thought. He picked up the little capsule curiously and placed it in the center of the bowl. Immediately he sensed heat rising from the metal chamber. Smoke wraiths curled up lazily from the capsule. He watched them with growing interest. The odor was heavy, hypnotic. Then, though the fumes continued to rise, the odor seemed to stop. Olfactory paralysis, he mused. But he had smelled enough to identify it. A cannabis derivative. He was going on a trip.

The voice resumed, and he listened dreamily.

"We have only the experiences and impressions of those who have 'died,' then returned to life. There are certain common features to these experiences. First, a spiritlike body seems to break away from the flesh-and-blood corpse. Hang on, Mrs. Welles!"

There was a wrench, and Quentin Thomas found himself leaving his body, which remained seated motionless at the console. He had one brief anxious moment, when he knew he was dead and that Ellen Welles had no one left to defend her. But his concern passed quickly as he floated freely through the ceiling of his booth, out through the roof, and over the chapel towers.

High in the air, his body began to move. He was floating and flying, without effort. The night lights of downtown Port City faded away, and he was in the suburbs. Then he was picking up speed. He found himself hurtling through a long tunnellike space. There was a light at the other end. As he burst through into the light, he heard music. It was gorgeous, sublime.

Something within his mind told him it was the most important music he would ever hear, the music of Fate. He knew those chords. He knew those transcendent strains. If only he could find the name.

As though buoyed up by the melody, he floated over a low, flat building surrounded by sweeping green lawns. There was something most peculiar about those lawns. Scattered over them were long light-reflecting gossamer strands. As he watched, a tractor sweeper passed under him, raking up the filaments.

He recognized it now. It was that nondescript building near the Universal Patents complex. He had seen it a couple of days earlier from the Chameleon.

Everything began to blur. The scenery slipped away. The music grew fainter and fainter, until finally it vanished altogether. The music of Fate. With infinite regret, he turned back.

There was a jolt. He was sitting in his chair once more, before the console.

"Welcome back, Mr. Thomas," the inner voice said.

He had to think about that. "How long have you known?" he asked.

"From the beginning."

"Why didn't you say so?"

"We wanted to respect your privacy as long as possible, Mr. Thomas."

"I see. Well, now that the mask is off, I have some questions."

"Of course."

"What is Fate?"

"Definitions are facile but generally meaningless."

"What *your* definition?"

"In general, Fate is an event rendered inevitable by an environmental matrix. The precise definition may depend on stimuli externally applied to the matrix."

Quentin Thomas almost smiled. A legal etymologist was loose in the circuits! "What was the music?" he said. "The Fate theme. Those musical notes?"

"Only you can say."

That was an interesting proposition. In fact, it was highly enlightening. "You mean, all this is from my own mind, my own experience? I have just been listening to myself think?"

"In a sense."

He was astonished.

"It's the new science of psychoelectronics, Mr. Thomas."

"Admirable," he murmured. "You are simply an aid to my own thought processes?"

"Pretty much."

"What were those strands of filament on the lawns around that building?"

"In good time, I think you may know. But you need more hard data. We can give back to you only your own input, peculiarly modified and enhanced by your current anxieties and interests—expressed and unexpressed."

We're now into the stock phrases, Quentin Thomas thought. He said, "You're not a hell of a lot of help, are you?"

"Possibly not. You must appreciate that there are great mysteries, and that all answers are but temporary compromises that fade eventually into ambiguities." There was a pause. "You are wondering about the intellects that programed some of my responses?"

"Yes."

"There were a number of us, Mr. Thomas. An exuberant man, a dying man, a woman in childbirth, a great religious figure, a well-known atheist. And many others. We help you think, Mr. Thomas. But we can't provide the true and final answers. We can't even suggest what questions you should ask."

"Will force of reason save Ellen Welles?"

"Lawyers like to think they can win a case by exercise of pure logic. Yet, as you of all people should appreciate, Mr. Thomas, there are two kinds of logic: winning logic and losing logic. The judge has to say which is which. And of course *he* can be wrong. You might never know for sure until you reach the Supreme Court. And even there you encounter frequent disagreement among the justices. Five might reason one way, four another. Who's right? The five. Except, of course, next time one of the five might join the minority of four, and then the former dissent becomes the new law of the land. 'We are not the court of last resort because we are infallible: We are infallible because we are the court of last resort.'"

"But does pure logic have any chance against Judge Speyer?" Thomas persisted.

"Yes—but with exceptions."

"Such as a no-appeal, capital punishment case?"

"Exactly."

"That's murder," Quentin Thomas said flatly.

"Yes. He needs to kill. What do *you* need, Mr. Thomas?"

"We weren't talking about me."

"Weren't we?"

He became defensive. "Every lawyer needs to win."

"Quite so, Mr. Thomas. For your opposition to win, Ellen Welles must die. For *you* to win—ah! Where would you draw the line?"

He was confused. "What?"

"Would you accept winning even if it meant Speyer must die?"

"I—yes, I guess, but—"

"And Kull and Ordway? Would you throw them in for good measure?"

He was listening to a hard, vindictive side of himself that he never knew existed. Yet there it was. "I never meant—I never said—"

He was retreating, but the other Quentin Thomas was in hot pursuit. "Suppose," the voice said, "that the three of them had to die, so that you could win?"

His teeth grated. "You don't have to put it that way."

"But it's true, isn't it, Mr. Thomas?"

"Yes," he whispered.

"I can barely hear you, counselor."

"YES!" he called out.

"And you're not so damn saintly, are you, Quentin Thomas?"

"No! I never claimed—" He noticed that he was on the verge of shouting. Abashed, he instantly subsided. It was time to quit. He removed the cap and rehung it on the wall peg. A burst of UV light bathed it momentarily. To sterilize it, he thought. But after what he had put it through, would it ever be sterile again?

The screen lit up. "Will that be all?"

"Yes," he said, exhausted.

"Would you like to make a contribution to the Chapel Maintenance Fund?"

He pushed his general credit card into the flashing slot. "Will a hundred be enough?"

"You are very generous. Please leave the cubicle door open as you go."

He opened the door and peered up the aisle. The place was empty. Either Ellen Welles had gone, or she was in one of the booths. He tiptoed to the side exit and left.

10

THE GAME OF SLEEP

It was midnight. He lay on his back in the semidarkness of his bedroom thinking about his session at Kirk Alloway and Ellen Welles and Fiber K, staring all the while at the sleep maze projected on his ceiling. For ten minutes his eyes had flickered along the borders, trying one alley after another. No luck.

He looked at the legend at the bottom, as though it might contain a clue. But all it said was "Copyright 2015, Sleep Enterprises, Inc." And below that, "A Sure Cure for Insomnia."

He shouldn't have taken the case. That woman would die, and it would be his fault. He twisted his shoulders. Of course, she would die anyway. But this way it was more nearly certain, and faster. By this time next Monday she would be dead.

Flicker . . . flicker . . . no solution. It was the first maze he had ever missed. Judge Speyer. That bastard. The hanging judge. Why did it have to be Speyer?

Ah . . . no . . . false lead.

Twice around the border now.

A legend at the top of the maze began to flash: "Ten minutes. Is this too difficult for you? Do you want the solution?"

"Go to hell," he growled.

There was a brief interval; then the whole maze began to flicker. On and off. On and off. A pattern. It's gone crazy, he thought. Probably inoperative. He watched it for a moment. Flicker, flicker, on and off.

He flipped off the projector and lay in the dark, staring at nothing. Perhaps into time. The seconds were ticking. Should he count the seconds? How many seconds until Ellen Welles's murder? Trial starts in the morning: Friday. Then the weekend. Saturday and Sunday to prepare for Monday. It would be all over on Monday. He'd try to string it out, delay, postpone. But Speyer wouldn't let him get away with any real delays. And then the end.

Stop thinking like that, counselor! Things to do. Check the files. Talk to the technical experts at Welles Engineering. Line up your witnesses. Check the progress of that *Williams* case, currently moving with slow certainty toward certiorari to the Supreme Court. Move for a continuance, based on *Williams,* first thing tomorrow.

He found himself thinking back to the flickering maze. On, off, on . . . Sleep Enterprises—wasn't that a spin-off from Universal Patents? The flickers—how had they gone? On, on, interval. On, on, on. Interval. On, long on, on, and again . . . and then he couldn't remember. But it was Morse code. "M . . . O . . . R . . . R . . ." MORRISSEY!

He hurriedly switched the maze back on. The flashing flickers started up again also immediately. "FIND MORRISSEY FIND MORRISSEY . . ."

It continued a few more seconds, then the whole image settled down to the original maze. Quentin Thomas shut it off and reached to his nighttable for his communicator mike.

"Legal Data."

"Yes, Mr. Thomas?"

"I want a listing of all amusement and/or educational devices licensed or manufactured by Universal Patents, together with a sublisting of all those involving active mental participation by adults. In each category, make a special indication of those that could involve secret encodings and those that appear to have been designed by Faust, the Universal Patents inventing computer."

"One moment, Mr. Thomas."

He counted forty seconds.

"Mr. Thomas?"

"Here."

"We can provide what you want, though we're not sure we have all material involving possible encodings. The list is lengthy and will require a printout at your terminal. It can begin in about thirty minutes. The price for what we can provide is $37,500."

"I'll take it."

"You have on deposit with us only $25,000."

He thought a moment. "I'm transferring $900,000 to my deposit account." He punched in the numbers in his bank hotline. It cleaned him out—checking and savings. He wondered if there'd be anything left after the trial.

"Your account is replenished, Mr. Thomas," the smooth metallic voice said. "The printout will soon begin."

He got into his bathrobe and walked into the den to watch the printout. Games, crossword puzzles, jigsaw puzzles. By the dozens, by the hundreds. All with the message, generally so cryptic you first had to know it was there: "Find Robert Morrissey." All designed by Faust, the inventing computer created by Robert Morrissey.

The implications were fascinating.

First there was Robert Morrissey, the remarkable inventor. *He* had designed Faust. Then, somewhere, somehow, Universal Patents had stepped in. Universal Patents now had title to Faust and to Faust's inventions, and was signing Faust's patents as administrator for Robert Morrissey, who was supposed to be insane. And Faust, in addition to an immense variety of industrial inventions, was cranking out educational fancies, almost as finger exercises. And all the oddities, in one way or another, kept repeating, "Find Morrissey." And that meant (1) Faust and Morrissey were separated; (2) Faust was concerned about Morrissey's well-being and location; (3) Faust was a living, thinking entity in his own right; (4) Finally, and perhaps most important, if (3) was true, then Faust, not Morrissey, was the true inventor of Fiber K, Morrissey was improperly named as the inventor on the patent and the patent was therefore invalid.

What could he do with all this? Nothing, unless he could find Robert Morrissey and/or get Faust into court. He spoke into the communicator. "Legal Data."

"Yes, Mr. Thomas?"

"Where is Robert Morrissey, the inventor of the inventing computer Faust?"

There was a long interval. Then the answer. "We don't know. No charge."

"Where is Faust?"

"One thousand dollars."

"Accepted."

"Faust is in a lead-lined building at Kay and Riviera Drive, Port City."

His head jerked. Parts of the puzzle were coming together. He tried to visualize the street patterns. Kay and Riviera. That's where U.P. had shot at the Chameleon. And small wonder—he had been hovering over Faust's building. That flat thing with the lawn. And the filamentary debris on the lawns. Filament . . . Faust . . . U.P. . . . what connection? What link with *U.P.* v. *Welles*? Eventually he would get it.

He pressed on. "Size?"

"Of Faust? One thousand."

"Accepted."

"Twenty-eight-thousand cubic feet."

Bigger than the courtroom, Thomas mused. Any way

to shrink Faust? Forget it! "Thank you, Legal Data, and good night."

"It is never night at Legal Data, Mr. Thomas, but goodnight to you, anyway."

He stood there, musing, frustrated. He needed Morrissey. He needed Faust. He needed something—but he couldn't name it. It was tucked away, deep down amid the sheltering folds of subconscious. He gave up.

On his way back to bed, he passed the music room. He paused and looked in. The Steinway stared back at him with allure. Tunes danced through his head. Tchaikovsky? (It was 1877. Tolstoy sat next to the great composer weeping, as they listened to the Andante of the D Major String Quartet. . . .) There was something, somewhere—he just couldn't focus on it—tied to Universal Patents, and Faust.

He needed help. A mirror to look into. And he knew where to find that mirror. Back to Kirk Alloway.

He returned to his dressing room, slipped out of his pajamas, and got into his street clothes. Fortunately the Kirk was just a couple of blocks down the street. Would it still be open at two in the morning? It had better be!

The night sky was clear; stars and a half moon lit the empty streets. He hurried along. He had forgotten his I.D. If a patrol picked him up there would be a problem. He might even spend the night in the slammer and miss the opening of the trial.

But here he was. He opened the chapel door and stepped inside quietly. As he expected, the place was empty. He walked back to the same booth, sat down, closed the door behind him, and put the cranial cap on his head. The audio greeted him promptly and cordially. "Good morning, Mr. Thomas."

"Good morning. And I have a question."

"Please proceed."

"I put it to you that each client makes a personality contribution to your psychographic data banks."

"That's true."

"So I'm in there, too? A part of me is registered in your data banks?"

"Yes."

"So that, in a sense, when I talk to you, I'm talking to myself?"

"Yes. We call it introspecting."

"Fine. I'd like to introspect."

"Go ahead. You are thinking about a life-and-death matter. You are searching for—"

"Robert Morrissey. Do I know where he is?"

"No. You don't know."

"Faust?" he persisted. "Does Faust know?"

"Very likely."

"How can I get Faust into the courtroom?"

"You can't. Too big."

"Is that final?"

"Just tentative. Nothing is final. Can you shrink Faust?"

Why was he there, jabbering away at a twisted, mocking version of himself? He might as well have stayed home. He should have gone to bed early. He should have saved his draining energies for corrosive confrontation with Speyer, just hours away.

"Why am I here?" he muttered plaintively.

"There is something else," came the soothing reply. "You knew the answers about Morrissey and Faust before you asked the questions. There's this other thing—the real reason you're here. Ask to look *deep*!" It was his own voice. And it was telling him that somewhere within his spirit was the final question, the final answer, and the final revelation.

He said evenly, "I'd like to see my face on the screen. I want it to show the basic question and answer that now elude me."

The screen slowly began to light up into roving patterns. Lines crossing and crisscrossing. Something was taking shape. A face? *His*? This strange apparition? The skin seemed wan, gray. The cheeks were sunken. Troubled eyes stared back at him.

What was his question? And where in this mask was the answer hidden?

He leaned closer and studied the face carefully. There was something in one of the eyes—a peculiar device, or symbol, wavering, dancing. For a moment it focused clearly and stood still for him:

Musical notes! How many? Seven?

They blurred and faded away.

Next the eyes went, then the cheeks, then the whole face.

Nothing was left on the screen.

Tantalizing. Seven notes. What did they mean? Absolutely nothing. Was it his fate to be mystified eternally, led astray, seduced into blind alleys? He had walked into the place with one mystery. He would walk out with several.

He was tired. He stood up and replaced the cap on its peg on the wall.

"Will that be all?" the audio asked.

"Yes," he said absently.

"Would you like to make a contribution to the Chapel Maintenance Fund?"

He pushed his card in the slot. "*I* should charge *you*."

"Beg pardon?"

"Here's a hundred." Seven musical notes, at about fourteen dollars a note. The high cost of music.

"Thank you, Mr. Thomas."

11

TRIAL DAY

On Friday morning, a large black electro moved smoothly and swiftly down Riviera Drive toward the Federal Building. On the righthand door was a tiny insigne, consisting of the words "Universal Patents" in gold, centered within a reticulated silver design that looked much like a spider web. That was the only breach in an otherwise sleek anonymity. In the back alcove, two men sat opposite the little foldout table, replacing papers in their attaché cases. They talked in low voices, more out of habit than to prevent the chauffeur from eavesdropping. Their privacy was ensured by the tinted dividing glass.

"I recognize the extreme importance of this Fiber K case against Welles Engineering," Jethro Kull said, "but I'm also concerned about the *Williams* case. Perhaps you should be in Washington, to handle that thing before the Supreme Court. Your man Jones could take over this Fiber K case until you get back."

"No," Ordway replied. "Practice before the Supreme Court requires a, ah, specialist—which I am not. In fact, there are only about a half-dozen firms in the country that I consider competent to handle *Universal Patents* v. *Williams*. With all due respect to Jones, I'm the best for this Welles case. I'm thoroughly prepared. The big thing in Welles is to persuade Speyer to find infringement before the, ah, high court can act in *Williams*."

"But will Speyer move it along?"

"Yes, I think so. He's got a crowded docket, and I hear by the grapevine that he's under immense pressure from the chief justice to get an opinion out in a big, ah, antitrust case that he's been sitting on for over a year. Of course, Quentin Thomas is sure to move for a continuance, to delay *Welles* until the Supreme Court decides *Williams*."

"What do you think Speyer would do with such a motion?"

"He'll deny it. I don't think he'll grant any continuance."

"Why not?"

"He's a total psycho. Our medical staff has given me a full report. He *needs*, ah, a guilty verdict. It recharges his mental batteries, gives him drive and the ability to work. We'll get all the breaks."

"Anything new on that fellow Thomas?"

"No. He turned us down, you know."

"Can you handle him, Ordway?"

"With a little help from Speyer, yes."

The limousine pulled into the driveway to the garage under the Federal Building. Jethro Kull barely noticed. He was thinking of other things. Years ago, when he had founded Universal Patents with Robert Morrissey, he had seen the foreshadowings of an international corporate colossus. If industry wanted to be competitive in the marketplace—if AT & T and General Motors and Dupont wanted to stay in business—they'd all have to come to him to take licenses under Faust's flood of new technology, and he would use the courts to enforce his patents.

This would be just the beginning. Already, U.P. was

the richest and most powerful corporation in the United States. His company had an income approximating the national military outlay. U.P. financed the election of senators and congressmen. The corporation was largely responsible for the election of the current President.

It was not enough.

In his mind, Jethro Kull envisioned abolition of the elective processes, at least at the national level. Within ten years, perhaps even five, he would own enough people in high places to pull it off. His Congress would pass the necessary bills. His President would sign them. His judges would support U.P. in the courts. Inevitably, U.P. would dismiss a forlorn, outdated, creaky, and inefficient system of government.

And long before that, the web of U.P. would have snatched up and devoured troublemakers such as this young idiot lawyer, what's-his-name.

But the fabulous future depended on the favorable outcome of cases in court. He absolutely had to win. His mind returned to the present. "Ordway," Kull said quietly, "just bear this in mind: If we lose this one, all of our licensees will rise in revolt. And if *that* happens, our royalty income vanishes, and Universal Patents will soon be bankrupt." He looked straight into the eyes of the lawyer. "Don't let that happen, Ordway."

His companion swallowed. "I understand Mr. Kull."

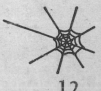

12

THE TRIAL BEGINS

The great room had ambience: a spacious serenity, rich walnut walls, high arched ceiling filled with light panels, a large rectangular slab of marble behind the bench. The law moved there with stately tread. "All rise," intoned the bailiff. "The United States District Court for Port City is now in session, the Honorable Rex Speyer presiding."

Judge Speyer entered from his chambers and strode rapidly toward the bench. He carried a large, thin portfolio that slapped at his robes as he climbed the three stairs to his big swivel chair. As soon as he was seated the clerk handed up the case file. He checked the caption briefly. *Universal Patents* v. *Welles*. Right case. He flicked his eyes about the room and spotted Ellen Welles instantly. Marvelous! They always brought in these terminal women, thinking to play on the sympathy of the jury. But he wasn't going to let this case go to the jury.

As if by some delayed reflex, his eyes returned to the woman. For a moment, he was puzzled. Do I know you? he thought. Have we met? The face was oddly, almost disconcertingly, familiar. Something about the sunken eyes, high cheekbones, the general emaciation . . . Who? When? Well, he grumped to himself, it'll either come to me or it won't. Perhaps a cocktail party somewhere. I meet a lot of people. No matter. Irrelevant.

Now, to get properly prepared. He opened the portfolio and took out his things. He knew his mode of relaxing at the bench sometimes provoked comment. But he didn't care. It was all very logical.

He was a rotund man, but his arms and legs were thin as sticks. His head seemed joined directly to his shoulders, without benefit of neck. Even as a boy he had had a round belly. His appearance and surname led quickly to his nickname, Spider. In adolescence, youth, and manhood he never lived it down. Even today it was not unusual for him to receive official mail addressed to Judge Spider.

Very well, then, The Spider. The opprobrium became first a challenge, and then a victory. Spiders had become his hobby. He lived spiders, even at the bench, even today, in this strange patent case. He looked down at the paper that he had pulled from his portfolio. It was his custom of long standing that, as he listened to the witnesses and the lawyers, he doodled.

Doodles? No, far too sophisticated to be doodles. Laid out flat before him on the bench, between the water carafe and bench case file, was his pad, measuring eleven by fourteen inches. On each sheet was a line drawing of a different spider. The arachnids were, of course, many times life size. The spread of legs could be a good six or eight inches. Sometimes the eight-legged creatures were shown on a segment of webbing. Sometimes they seemed to run freely on the ground, betwixt pebble and fallen twig. Sometimes they dangled from a single tiny silken thread. The plates were prepared by the New England Arachnid Society. What a job they were doing! Nearly seven hundred species had been identified in New England. The Society published this set of line drawings in three volumes; the buyer was supposed to color the drawings according to a code provided on the plate.

And what have we here today? Atropos. A newly discovered species, evidently a mutant from Klotho via Lachesis. Only one hundred specimens known to exist. He had one, of course. In the terrarium in his bachelor quarters. There was something special about the filament. Atropos could sense when its web had caught a fly because of tiny electric currents that went up the core of the silk to the nerve center of the web. Or so they said.

As soon as things got going, he would dip the watercolor brush in the little water well, touch the brush to the cake of cobalt blue, and begin filling in the central band around Atropos's abdomen. And then the two bands of vermilion. Blue and red, like his mother's bathrobe . . . which she hadn't been wearing . . . that time. And why on Earth should he now remember his mother's blue-and-red striped bathrobe? Dead these ten years. Love, hate—he never knew which, for her, or for him. The mind plays strange tricks. No matter, madame, during this upcoming morning session we will proceed to cover your nudity properly.

Once more, with great satisfaction, he sought out the head and eyes of Ellen Welles. He no longer worried where he had seen her before. Perhaps at his mother's farewell garden party, before she left for Switzerland. He had attended the festivities for a few minutes, unseen.

He looked at Ellen Welles. Good, good. He couldn't ask for better. He thought about his antitrust case, *U.S.* v. *Systems Motors*. It was as good as written. This woman would die, and watching her die would give him the mental energy he needed for *Systems*. His *Systems* opinion would turn out to be a major contribution to antitrust law. The law review journals would analyze it for months. He rubbed his hands together with great satisfaction. Hang in there, Milady Atropos, it's going to be a fine day.

He swiveled his high-backed chair toward the jury box. "I am required by law to make this opening statement to you. You, the jury, are sitting in an action for patent infringement. Counsel for plaintiff, Mr. Ordway, in the green robe, sits at the table nearest you. Counsel for defendant, Mr. Thomas, in the red robe, sits at the far table. In addition, at defendant's table sits a person dressed in black. This person is called an oblate, and I will come to that." He surveyed his courtroom. Packed. Observers could get in only by special ticket. He had seen the rules drawn up by the Committee of Clerks. First, representatives of eighteen foreign patent offices. Then the bar association selections, then about two dozen amici curiae. Then the technical associations: the ACS, AiChE, ASME—the whole alphabet soup schmear. The NAM wanted to enjoin the further operation of the invention machine as destroying the national economy. The Department of Justice wanted to put all the machine's inventions in the public domain. The Commissioner of Patents had filed a three-hundred page a.c. urging invalidity of the Patent Office's own patent. Odd. Not that it mattered. And then, the press. And finally of course, the TV crews, who would carry the whole incredible mess to a quarter billion viewers all over the world.

He continued. "Approximately four hundred suits for patent infringement were brought in the federal courts in the last decade of the twentieth century. Every one of the patents involved was found invalid. In most of the cases, the plaintiff was required to pay all costs, including fees of defense counsel. As a consequence, not one complaint for patent infringement was filed in the first year of the present century. In fact, during that period, patent applications filed in the U.S. Patent Office dropped by nearly ninety-five percent. The patent system, so long a cornerstone of our pattern of free enterprise and innovation, was dead."

Quentin Thomas looked at the thirteen faces on the jury, including the alternate, a pleasant-looking grandmother. Did any of them understand what Speyer was telling them? Six men, six women, and the alternate. Working people. Retirees. Housewives. That pregnant woman. How in God's name did she ever get on the jury list?

"The Congress responded," the judge went on, "by passing the Patent Act of 2002. This new patent act makes two drastic changes in the former patent laws. First, the defendant is presumed guilty of the charge of infringement until he proves his innocence. Second, patent infringement is a criminal offense: It carries the death penalty."

A loud buzzing suddenly burst up from the room, like a swarm of noisy insects taking flight. Judge Speyer banged the bench with his gavel. As the drone died away, he spoke succinctly. "I will have an orderly court. If I find that is not possible, the public will be excluded."

At the sudden quiet, he paused to reflect on his gavel. It was a special, very satisfactory gavel. The end of the handle was fitted with two yellowed butterfly-shaped objects, spaced a little apart from each other: two vertebrae from the neck of Estelle Johnson, the last woman to be hanged in the United States. The fall through the trapdoor broke the neck and the spinal chord. Death was instantaneous. And so death had snapped apart these two sturdy fragments; and so he had paid well for them. Interesting, but entirely too humane. He didn't like instantaneous deaths. The condemned should show something, some awareness of his changing condition. He or she should know what was happening, and should make some minimal response. That was fifty percent of the show. The British had the right idea. Kick the little stool out from under. The person fell just a few inches; when the execution was skillfully arranged, his toes actually touched the floor. His neck stretched, his eyes popped, his face turned purple. He danced his little jig. Gave him time to think.

"As originally proposed," Speyer continued, "the

new patent act designated the chief executive of the
infringer as the party subject to the death penalty. It
was evident that Congress had in mind a corporation
president or chairman of the board. As the subsequent
case law developed, however, it became clear that the
penalty was assignable. All the company president
needed to do was to find a person willing to assume
the risk. We call this person the *oblate*." He studied
his notes for a moment, then looked over toward the
defense table. "Mrs. Welles?"

Ellen Welles started to rise. "No," Thomas whispered. "Just say, 'Yes, Your Honor,' and answer his
questions."

She sat down nervously. "Yes, Your Honor."

"You are the oblate?"

"Yes."

"You understand that if a verdict of infringement is
found, you will be required to drink a solution of one
gram of potassium cyanide dissolved in water?"

"I understand, Your Honor."

"And if you should be adjudged guilty but refuse
to drink the solution, you will be physically restrained,
and you will then die by forcible injection of cyanide.
Do you understand that?"

"Yes, Your Honor."

"Alas," Speyer said unctuously, "we are required
to place a price on that which is priceless. So I must
ask you, have you posted the required bond for your
appearance here, each and every day of this trial?"

"I have, Your Honor."

"This bond is all assets of Welles Engineering Corporation?"

"It is, Your Honor."

"If you should fail to appear, you understand that
your bond will be forfeit, and in addition, you must still
drink the poison, and finally, failing that, you must die
by forcible injection of cyanide?"

"Yes."

"This trial may require two, possibly three days. Do
you expect to live that long?"

"So I am told by my doctors, Your Honor."

He studied the medical report in the case file. Her doctors gave her one to six months. The point was crucial. She had to live long enough for him to pronounce sentence. She had to live long enough to die. Interesting paradox. He wondered if she would appreciate it. Probably not. "You will be survived by—"

"A daughter, Your Honor. Age thirteen."

"Yes. I see. Well, then, I pronounce you to be a satisfactory oblate. You must now wear a hood at all times during these proceedings. Have you brought your own, or do you want the bailiff to provide one?"

Quentin Thomas handed her the black hood.

"I have my own, Your Honor." She pulled it over her head like a loose flimsy ski mask and looked up at Speyer through half-hidden eyes.

"Let's get on with it," Speyer said. He looked over the dais to the bailiff. The bailiff nodded. Speyer continued. "At this point, by virtue of Local Rule of Court Number One Forty, we shall have The Test. Bailiff, are you prepared to carry out The Test?"

"I am, Your Honor."

"Raise your right hand."

The bailiff raised his right hand.

"Do you swear to make The Test faithfully and in accordance with law?"

"I do."

"Please proceed, describing each step for the record."

"Yes, Your Honor." He pulled on a pair of rubber gloves, and his voice shifted into a sort of sing-song. "First I mix out eight fluid ounces of distilled water into this drinking glass. Then I take this weighing balance. I set the scales at one gram, and I place a filter paper on the weighing pan. Then I take this brown bottle, which contains chemically pure potassium cyanide in the form of a white powder, and I shake out enough potassium cyanide onto the filter paper to make the scale balance. Then I empty the contents of the paper into the glass of water, and stir with this glass rod until it is all dissolved."

Quentin Thomas looked at the masked woman from the corner of his eye. He knew she was watching with rapt attention, but he could only guess at the expression on her face. Was it fascination? Fear? Horror?

"That," the bailiff said, "is part one of The Test. Next, from the glass I pour a little of the solution into this little dish, and in a moment I shall slide the dish into this cage." He motioned to a screened cage on a serving cart. "The cage contains a mouse that has had nothing to drink for three days. Owing to the requirements of confinement, a closed-circuit TV system will show events within the cage not otherwise visible." The lights within the courtroom dimmed as a picture lit up the far wall opposite the jury box.

In the picture was a mouse—many times life size. The tray of poison-water was pushed through a slit in the front of the cage. The little creature drew back at first, then sniffed in the direction of the liquid. An eerie silence fell over the courtroom. The mouse crept forward slowly, fearfully, put its head over the lip of the dish, drank a sip or two, backed off, collapsed, and expired amid convulsions that knocked over the drinking dish.

The bailiff opened the top of the cage, picked up the little mammal by the tail between gloved thumb and forefinger, and showed the test product first to the judge, then to the jury.

"Thank you, bailiff," Judge Speyer said.

Quentin Thomas had seen it all once before. It had revolted him then, and it revolted him now, to the point that his hands trembled. The death of the mouse wasn't what got to him. Nor even the possibility that Ellen Welles might have to drink from that glass. No, what threatened to dissolve his intestines was a tiny sliver of saliva making its way down Judge Speyer's chin. And the way Speyer was staring at Ellen Welles. As if Speyer were a boa constrictor coiling slowly toward a hypnotized rabbit.

Life seemed to flow back into the room. The bailiff dropped the test animal back into its cage, walked to the chrome-lined glass box that contained the poison drink, closed the lid, snapped the lock, and placed the assembly on the judge's bench, next to the coloring book. He then wheeled the mouse cart out of the room. Judge Speyer turned to the jury with a smile. "At this point it is customary to mention that a sterile hypodermic syringe rests in its plastic sheath, next to the aqueous cyanide."

The bastard! Quentin Thomas thought. He's looking straight at Ellen!

"To be used, of course, only in the event of forcible restraint. And that completes The Test. I trust we are all impressed with the solemnity of the occasion. So, let us get on with the trial."

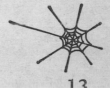

13

THE TRIAL CONTINUES

This moment, Quentin Thomas thought, is like the last seconds before the start of a horse race. Just now, in this one precious fleeting moment, all things are possible. A fifty-to-one shot could still win. Disaster has not yet crystallized. It's like the minutes preceding the bar exam. The questions haven't yet been handed out. Vague formless hopes loomed over the horizon. Enjoy this moment, counselor! Revel in these euphoric milliseconds! They will never return!

Judge Speyer looked over at plaintiff's table. "We'll start with motions. Mr. Ordway?"

Ordway stood up. "No motions, Your Honor."

"Mr. Thomas?"

Defense counsel pushed his chair back, flicked his red robe aside, and got to his feet. "Your Honor, I move to postpone this trial until the United States Supreme Court decides *Universal Patents* versus *Williams.* As your honor is probably aware, *Williams* is a patent infringement case similar in its facts to this instant litigation, and with the same plaintiff. In *Wil-*

liams the defendant lost but moved for a stay of execution pending review by the Court of Appeals for the Ninth Circuit. The Court of Appeals, however, refused to hear the appeal, noting that the language of the patent statute gave no right of appeal. Thereupon defendant petitioned certiorari to the Supreme Court to review the single question of whether denial of appeal rendered the entire statute unconstitutional. The present posture of that case is that the petition for certiorari is before the high court and the court is expected to decide within the next few days whether it will grant the petition. If it grants the petition, as is indeed anticipated, the Supreme Court may be expected to hand down its decision the following day."

"Mr. Ordway?" Speyer said.

"Well, Your Honor, I oppose, of course. In the first place, there is no firm evidence that the Supreme Court has the petition before it. But assuming it has docketed the petition and will vote in due course on whether to grant it, it is sheer speculation on our part that the high court would find the patent statute unconstitutional. I respectfully submit that such possibility is highly unlikely. Considering the remoteness of the possibility, a continuance is not justified. So I oppose."

"For the moment, Mr. Ordway, I'll agree with you. I deny defendant's motion for a continuance. However, Mr. Thomas, I grant you leave to renew your motion if and when the Supreme Court does in fact grant certiorari to *Universal Patents* v. *Williams*."

"That may be too late, Your Honor," Thomas protested. "It's just a matter of a few days. Surely this case can wait two or three days? I ask Your Honor to reconsider."

"Let the record show that I have reconsidered," Speyer said coolly, "but without changing my decision. Your motion is denied, Mr. Thomas."

"Yes, Your Honor." He sat down. He had expected nothing else.

"Now then," Speyer continued, "does plaintiff have an opening statement?"

"Yes, Your Honor." Ordway swept his green robe around his body in an elegant swirl as he rose to face the jury. "Ladies and gentlemen, as Judge Speyer has told you, this is a patent infringement suit. By the simple act of, ah, filing a complaint in this court, my client, Universal Patents, establishes a presumption that the defendant, Welles Engineering Corporation, infringes our patent. Our patent covers a remarkable synthetic fiber, remarkable in that it conducts electric current. The Welles Corporation makes and sells such a fiber, which they call Fiber K, and thereby they are presumed to infringe our patent. This presumption is rebuttable. By this we mean that it's up to Welles to show that they don't infringe, or that our patent is invalid." He paused to cast a contemptuous glance toward the defense table. "They have hired a very brilliant lawyer, Mr. Quentin Thomas, who will try very hard to convince you that our patent is indeed invalid, or not infringed, or both. But we think you will find that the evidence he will adduce is, ah, insufficient." He looked down at his tabletop and coughed delicately. "Now, as Judge Speyer has told you, patent infringement carries the death penalty. If the defendant loses, sentence is passed, and the person designated as the oblate will die before your very eyes. Don't let this possibility influence your thinking, ladies and gentlemen, especially since Mrs. Welles is, ah, terminal and due to die from natural causes any day, any hour. Thank you." He bowed to the jury, then to Speyer, and sat down.

"Mr. Thomas?" Speyer asked.

"No opening statement, Your Honor."

"Very well then. Call your first witness."

The defense lawyer looked out over the sea of faces. "I call Ronald Flagman."

A man rose from the audience, pushed his way to the aisle, and strode up through the courtroom toward the witness stand, where the bailiff swore him in. He stepped up into the stand.

"Please state your name," Thomas said.

"Ronald Flagman."

"What is your current employment?"

"Commissioner of Patents, United States Patent Office."

"Mr. Flagman, in your capacity as Commissioner of Patents, do you receive patent applications from inventors throughout the world?"

"I do."

"I show you a copy of Plaintiff's Exhibit One for identification, United States Patent 6,005,022, and I ask you to note the name of the inventor."

"On the face of the patent," Flagman replied, "it states, 'Robert Morrissey, by his Administrator, Universal Patents.' "

"Are you aware that the actual inventor is a computer-machine named Faust?"

Ordway was on his feet. Objection! The question assumes several facts not in evidence, namely that something called Faust exists; that Faust is capable of invention; that Faust did in fact make the invention in question; and that Mr. Morrissey did not make the invention."

Speyer looked up from his coloring book. "Sustained."

Quentin Thomas smiled faintly. "Have you ever heard of something called Faust?"

"Yes."

"In what connection?"

"I've read the newspaper and journal articles. I've heard the commentator reports on TV and radio."

"Do these reports describe Faust as an inventing computer?"

"Objection," Ordway said. "Leading."

"Sustained," Speyer agreed.

"Mr. Flagman," Thomas persisted, "how do these reports describe Faust?"

"Objection, hearsay."

"What the witness has heard with his own ears is admissible, Your Honor," Thomas said. He added smoothly, "I offer not for the truth of what he heard, but for the fact that he heard it." If he got the point in at all, under any guise, he knew—and Ordway knew —that the jury wasn't going to keep this subtle distinction in mind.

"Objection overruled," Speyer said. "You may answer, if you know. Will the reporter repeat the last question?"

Ordway flashed a piercing glance of hatred at Quentin Thomas, who smiled back.

The reporter held up a length of paper tape from his steno machine and read: "Mr. Flagman, how do these reports describe Faust?'"

"As an inventing computer," the patent commissioner said.

"Do the reports say anything else?"

"Yes. According to the reports, Faust was assembled by Robert Morrissey and Faust files a great many patent applications in the Patent Office."

"Is this also *your* understanding, Mr. Flagman?"

"Objection," Ordway said. "It has not been established that the witness has personal knowledge that anything was assembled. Also, the question, as phrased, is compound."

"Sustained."

"Mr. Flagman," Thomas continued, "does the Patent Office receive a great many patent applications from Robert Morrissey by his administrator, Universal Patents?"

"Yes."

"Can you explain in a general way what procedures the Patent Office follows in examining the patent applications it receives from Universal Patents?"

"The same as for all applications, Mr. Thomas."

"Which is?"

Ordway stood again. "Your Honor, I object to this line of questioning as irrelevant. The internal mechanisms of the Patent Office have nothing to do with validity or infringement."

"Will counsel approach the bench," Speyer said.

When they arrived, the judge spoke to Quentin

Thomas. "He's right, Mr. Thomas. Is this leading to anything?"

"Yes, Your Honor. I'm attempting to show a couple of things. First, that the standard Patent Office procedures make no effort to determine inventorship, that indeed they have no facilities to make such an investigation. They have to take whatever is told them. Second, that their research mechanisms are inadequate to cope with Faust."

Speyer looked down the room at the hooded woman. "I'm going to let you continue, Mr. Thomas, but I'm going to require that you keep it down to the bare bones. Don't ask the commissioner whether he is aware what Justice Jackson said about patents, or Abe Lincoln, or Thomas Jefferson."

"No, Your Honor," the lawyer said dryly. He resumed his examination of the commissioner. "The pending question was directed to the general procedures used by the Patent Office. What happens when the office receives a patent application?"

"First, our clerks check each application to make sure that all the parts are there: specification, claims, declaration of inventorship by the applicant, and the filing fee. If the cover letter mentions drawings, the receiving section verifies the number of sheets of drawings."

"What next?"

"The application is routed to the classification branch. There, technical experts determine what technology it relates to. For example, is it electrical, chemical, agricultural, and so on. Following this determination, it is routed to the proper group for examination."

"What happens when it reaches the proper group?"

"It is subclassified. Which is to say, within that group it is assigned to the patent examiner who handles the exact art in question. Say it goes to the organic chemistry group. Well, there you have a further breakdown into dyes, polymers, steroids, and so on. The designated examiner puts it at the bottom of his stack, figuratively speaking. He takes up his cases in turn. When a case comes up for examination, he makes a search to determine if it is novel and unobvious."

"How does he make this search?"

"There are two methods: hand search and machine search. He might use either or both. It's up to him, at his discretion."

"What is the hand search?"

"The examiner looks at certain select files in the group search room. We call these files shoes. Some of them are extremely extensive and go far beyond what we have in the public search room on the main floor of the Patent Office."

"And how about a machine search?"

"That's simply done by computer. The examiner can plug in several key words, such as polyamide, electrically conductive, and so on, and see what references the computer can extract from its data banks."

"What represents the general input into the data banks of the Patent Office computer?"

"It is fairly broad. We have a reciprocity arrangement with all the patent offices of the examining countries throughout the world. Also we have the major technical journals."

"Have you heard any reports regarding Faust's data bank?"

"Yes."

"How does the Patent Office computer compare as regards data bank input?"

The commissioner shrugged. "We have studied that. Our estimate is that we get about one third of the technology, and that our time lag in getting it into our computer is about ten months, as compared to no lag at all for Faust."

"Please explain, Mr. Flagman."

"Well, the technical-journal budget of the Patent Office Scientific Library gives us access to about one third of the journals available to Faust."

"But how about the time lag? Are you saying it takes

the Patent Office ten months to get data out of a given journal and into your computer?"

"Yes. This is done by a group of professional abstractors. They read the journals, abstract what they think important, and transfer it to the computer data bank library. Faust, of course, has a built-in reader. He scans the literature electronically. His input is instantaneous."

"*His* input, Mr. Flagman?"

"I spoke figuratively, Mr. Thomas."

"Can't the Patent Office install an electronic reader?"

"We have been looking for one. Actually, you can't just go out and buy one off the shelf. To have a reader designed and manufactured specifically for the Patent Office computer would cost about ten million dollars. We have asked for this money in our budgets submitted for each of the past five years, but so far Congress has not seen fit to give it to us."

"In what year was the first application filed by Mr. Morrissey?"

"So far as our records show, it was 2003."

"Did Mr. Morrissey sign the declaration himself, or was it executed by his guardian, Mr. Kull?"

"Mr. Morrissey signed it himself."

"Did he make that invention by the use of Faust?"

"I don't know."

"When did Mr. Kull start signing as administrator for Mr. Morrissey?"

The commissioner checked his notes. "In 2005."

"How many patent applications did Mr. Kull file that year, as Mr. Morrissey's administrator?"

"Ninety-six."

"And how many did he file last year?"

"About twenty thousand."

"What was the total for all patent applications filed last year?"

"Twenty thousand, five hundred."

"So he filed about ninety-seven percent of all the patent applications received by the Patent Office last year?"

"Yes."

"Mr. Flagman, have you had occasion to check with foreign patent offices on this point? By this I mean, is it also the experience of the foreign patent offices that Universal Patents is filing most of the patent applications that are being filed in their countries?"

"Yes. It is approximately the same, at least in the countries that have an enforceable patent system." He looked at his notes. "In Japan, ninety percent of the applications are filed by Universal Patents; in West Germany, ninety-five percent; in the United Kingdom, ninety-four percent—"

Ordway stood up. "Your Honor, I object to this line of questioning. The percentages of patent applications filed by plaintiff throughout the world are completely irrelevant to the two central issues in this case, which are: Is the fiber patent valid, and does defendant infringe it? Even if one could predict that Universal Patents will file one hundred percent of the patents that are filed starting next year, and even if you assume that Universal Patents will, ah, eventually own all new and useful technology by next year, it would all be irrelevant to any issue in this case."

"Objection sustained," Speyer agreed. "The jury is instructed to ignore defendant's line of questioning involving plaintiff's percentage participation in world patent filings."

Quentin Thomas lifted his shoulders very slightly. So much for monopolization of the Patent Office by Universal Patents. But he had by no means exhausted Flagman's possibilities. "Mr. Flagman, did the Patent Office file an amicus brief in this case?"

"We did."

"Who actually wrote it?"

"I did."

"Did you make a recommendation?"

"Yes, sir."

"What was it?"

"We asked that the court find the fiber patent invalid."

"Invalid? On what basis does the Patent Office think one of its own duly issued patents is invalid?"

"Objection," Ordway said. "Mr. Flagman's answer will be conclusory and speculative."

"Overruled," Speyer responded. "You may answer, Mr. Flagman."

"The Patent Office has contended for several years that patents generated by a computer, especially by a program based on negative selection, are invalid."

"Objection," Ordway said. "The question assumes as a fact that Faust, as a computer, not Morrissey as a human being, made the Fiber K invention."

"Not at all," Quentin Thomas countered. "The question is simply directed to a procedural point within the Patent Office."

"Objection overruled," Speyer said. "You may answer, if you know."

"Well, in our treatment of computer-associated inventions in the Patent Office, we are necessarily guided by two milestone decisions. We call them Morrissey I and Morrissey II."

"Perhaps you'd better take those up one at a time," suggested Thomas. "What was involved in Morrissey I?"

"The issue there was whether a patent could be granted on a machine search reporting output in terms of negative selection."

"Explain negative selection."

"One example would be this. Suppose the literature shows a certain process performed using methanol, ethanol, and butanol, but with no mention of propanol. By the process of negative selection the computer selects propanol, which of course lies between ethanol and butanol in the homologous series of alkanols. That's the computer's new invention, carrying out the old process, but using propanol. And that's what we in the Patent Office call negative selection."

"Does negative selection require the abstract act of invention?"

"In my opinion, no."

"Has negative selection ever been tested in court?"

"Yes. That's what we call Morrissey I. It originated as *Ex parte Morrissey*, before the Patent Office Board of Appeals, in 2005. The Board held that as a matter of law, negative selection could not qualify as invention. The claims were rejected. Universal Patents appealed to the Court of Customs and Patent Appeals, which reversed the Patent Office and held that negative selection *could* qualify as the inventive act. The CCPA spelled this out in 2006. First, they required the Patent Office to look at the invention as defined in the claims, without regard to whether the invention had been made by a computer or directly by human intuition. Second, the decision held that the process of negative selection does not in itself destroy invention."

"Has the Patent Office rejected any of Faust's patent applications since that time?"

"Yes, on several occasions."

"On what grounds?"

"Well, after Morrissey I, we abandoned negative selection as a basis for rejection. Thereafter, the ground was obviousness."

"What do you mean by obviousness?"

"We relied on the definition in the patent statute, to the effect that, if the differences in the claimed invention and the closest prior art were such that the invention would be obvious to one skilled in the art, the alleged invention was unpatentable."

"A subjective judgment?"

"Yes."

"What happened to Faust's applications that you rejected for obviousness?"

"Universal Patents abandoned about half. The other half, they took to the CCPA. They got reversals in about thirty percent of their appeals."

"How do those numbers compare with your averages for other inventors?"

"About the same, although you must appreciate the remaining inventors are fewer in number and present a much smaller sample."

"Now, Mr. Flagman, you testified that the Patent Office has, or had, a computer capable of making a machine search of the prior art. Have you ever tried to extend its capability?"

"Yes. We had it modified in an attempt to turn it into an inventing computer."

"How did you do that?"

"Well, for one thing, we hard-wired it to use the principle of negative selection."

"But hadn't the CCPA already instructed the Patent Office not to reject on negative selection?"

"Yes, but this was different. We wanted to *demonstrate* that any computer, properly modified, could come up with inventions resulting from the principle of negative selection and that, therefore, the alleged invention lay within the public domain and could not be the subject of a monopoly."

"Proceed. What result?"

"We had problems. In the first place, as I have already mentioned, our machine did not have nearly the data bank resources that Faust had. Also, there was a severe time lag in our case. The modifications proved inadequate to prove our point. To cope with Faust, we needed another Faust—a twin—at a cost far beyond our means, even assuming that we had Mr. Morrissey available to build it for us. We disconnected the modification several years ago. The basic computer will still make a routine machine search, but it doesn't try to invent anymore."

"Why not?"

"Because of Morrissey II."

"What about Morrissey II?"

"Faust filed a patent application on a new alloy. Our modified machine searched the literature. The new alloy wasn't in the literature. It was at least literally novel. We then tried the concept of negative selection on our machine. We assumed that it was by this procedure that Faust conceived the new alloy, by adding a metal component that the prior art had missed."

"And did your machine find the missing metal?"

"No, our machine missed it. But we rejected the patent application anyhow, on the general ground of obviousness."

"What happened next?"

"Universal Patents appealed. First to the Patent Office Board of Appeals. The Board confirmed the Examiner's rejection. And then Universal appealed to the CCPA."

"The Court of Customs and Patents Appeals," Quentin Thomas said. "What happened there?"

"They reversed us."

"On what grounds?"

"Well, this is the famous decision in Morrissey II, which I mentioned earlier. The court said that since Faust had found the alloy, and since the Patent Office computer, though wired to invent, had *failed* to find it, this was clear evidence that Faust—or Morrissey—had transcended the skill of the art, and they held the alloy unobvious."

"They were using the inadequacies of your machine as proof of unobviousness of Faust's invention?"

"Objection, leading."

"Overruled."

"That's the way it looked to us at the Patent Office," the commissioner said.

"And that's why you disconnected the modification to your computer?"

"Exactly. We simply returned it to its normal examining function."

"Thank you, Mr. Flagman. I have no further questions." He returned to his table, aware that Ellen Welles's eyes were searching his face through the slits in her hood. There was nothing to say. Had he been able to cast a little doubt as to the validity of the fiber patent in the mind of at least one jury member?

"Any cross, Mr. Ordway?" Speyer asked.

"Just a couple of questions, Your Honor." He walked up to the podium, his green robes trailing in grandeur. "Mr. Flagman, does the Patent Office computer have a mind, a being, a soul of its own?"

"Not that I know of."

"It's just a very intricate piece of electronic hardware?"

"Yes."

"As is every computer?"

"Yes, so far as I know."

"You have mentioned hearing reports about a computer named Faust?"

"Yes."

"And you've mentioned reports to the effect that one Robert Morrissey invented Faust?"

"Yes."

"And that Faust is supposed to have invented applications being filed in the Patent Office by, ah, Robert Morrissey?"

"I've heard that."

"As a philosophical point, Mr. Flagman, as between Morrissey and Faust, who is the inventor of inventions flowing from Faust?"

"Objection, speculation," Thomas said.

"Mr. Flagman's opinion is asked as an expert in the field of invention," Ordway retorted. "There's no speculation."

"Objection overruled," Speyer said. "You may answer, Mr. Flagman, but you must give the basis for your conclusion."

"As between Morrissey and Faust, Morrissey is the inventor, and the reason is, Faust is but a machine conceived and assembled by Morrissey. When Faust speaks, it is actually Morrissey speaking."

Damn! Thomas thought. Good point, and it's going to hurt. He ignored Ordway's twisted triumphant smile.

"That's all I have," Ordway said.

"Redirect, Mr. Thomas?" Speyer asked.

"Yes, Your Honor." He addressed the Commissioner of Patents. "Mr. Flagman, suppose Mr. Morrissey were dead, but his computer continues to invent as programmed. Is Mr. Morrissey the inventor of these posthumous inventions?"

Ordway jumped up. "Now *that's* speculation, Your Honor! I object!"

"It's directed to Mr. Flagman's opinion as an expert in the field of invention, to use Mr. Ordway's words," Quentin Thomas said.

Speyer shrugged. "Overruled. Answer if you can, Mr. Flagman."

"Mr. Morrissey would still be the inventor," the commissioner said.

The defense lawyer pressed on. "Now, suppose Faust keeps inventing. It's now ten years after Morrissey's death. No one modifies Faust's circuits. He's just as Morrissey designed him. Is Morrissey still the inventor of Faust's output?"

"Yes. The cases would be filed in the name of his estate, of course, by his personal representative."

"Make that one hundred years later, Mr. Flagman. Who's the inventor?"

"Morrissey," the patent official said doggedly.

"One thousand years, Mr. Flagman?"

"I think we are moving into a very unclear area, sir."

"Well, let's try to clear it up, Mr. Flagman. Is Mr. Morrissey, through his computer, immortal?"

"I don't think I can answer that, Mr. Thomas."

"So there might be a dividing line? A point in time at which Morrissey ceases to be the inventor, and after that, Faust is the inventor?"

"Possibly."

"Can you say with absolute certainty that that point had not been reached when Faust filed the patent application for Fiber K?"

"No, I can't."

"So Faust might possibly have been the true and sole inventor of Fiber K?"

"I don't know, Mr. Thomas. I just don't know."

"I appreciate the difficulties here, Mr. Flagman. Let's get back to well-known legal principles. If Faust *were* the sole inventor, and not Morrissey, would the patent be valid?"

"No, in that case it would be invalid. The correct inventor has to be named."

"Thank you, Mr. Flagman. I have nothing further."

"Re-cross, Mr. Ordway?" Speyer asked.

"No, Your Honor."

"You may stand down, Mr. Flagman," Speyer said. "And now, since it's approximately noon, we'll have a recess. The court will adjourn until one thirty."

"All rise,," the bailiff intoned. "This honorable court is now in recess."

After Speyer had left the room, Quentin Thomas helped Ellen Welles remove her mask.

"What do we do with this thing?" she asked.

"I'll keep it in my attaché case," he said gravely. "You'll need it again when trial resumes. Local rule something or other." He removed his robe and stuffed it into the case along with her hood. Then he looked at her, full in the face, almost accusingly. "He recognized you."

"What? Who?"

"Speyer. The way his eyes opened when he first saw you. He came in, climbed up the stairs to his chair, and then he looked over at you. His chin jerked. He knows you."

"No, I don't think it's possible. Really."

"Ellen, I have to know everything. If you knew him at some time in the past, in any context whatever, I have to know."

"But Quentin, I *didn't*. He's a complete stranger."

He studied her face. Her protesting gray eyes bored back at him. She seemed to be telling the truth. That meant the recognition, if it had been, was entirely unilateral, and probably even in error. Perhaps the doomed woman had reminded His Honor of someone. It was something to think about.

"What now?" she asked.

"Let's go out for a bite to eat."

14

THE TRIAL, CONTINUED

Ellen Welles stared gloomily into her cup of soup. "I guess we didn't do too well with Flagman."

"No," Quentin Thomas said. "But then, he didn't know very much. What we did get from him was the official position of the Patent Office, that the Fiber K patent is invalid."

She was silent. He read her clearly. She was evaluating him, and she was disappointed. She was thinking that everything would be lost. The plant would go. Nothing would be left for Lorie And what comfort could he give her? None, really. Their chances, never good, had not improved with the morning. But he couldn't tell her that. She relied on him to *win*. God! Why hadn't he gone into banking, medical malpractice, corporate work? Why this hopeless, insane patent program?

He thought of the way Speyer had watched Ellen Welles. Spider and fly. Come in, little fly. Closer, closer. That's fine, buzz a bit for me. I like the buzzing —stimulates my salivaries.

What was wrong with Speyer? he mused. Did it have a name? Was it a "sacrifice-to-the-gods" complex? He thought back into history. Agamemnon slew his daughter Iphegenia to gain a fair wind for the Greek fleet. Xerxes sacrificed nine Greek youths to inspire his generals in the invasion of Hellas. On occasions of divine communion the Aztec priests would cut the heart out of a living man and offer it up to their god. And he once knew a clergyman who volunteered to operate the vacuum chamber at the dog pound on Friday nights. On Saturday that man would return to his office in his church and write his Sunday sermon.

Speyer had it bad. But it wasn't just Speyer.

What is this dark and terrible thing within us? Quentin Thomas wondered. He didn't know. He wanted *not* to know.

"Speyer seemed fair enough," Ellen Welles said. "He listened to everything. He made reasoned rulings."

How can I tell her Thomas, thought. It's his facade, an illusion that he deliberately creates, a hope that he builds up in his victims. It improves the shock value of his ultimate death sentence.

"We don't have much time for lunch," he said. "You'd better eat something."

"I'm not hungry. Who are you going to call as your next witness?"

"Jethro Kull."

Her eyes widened. "You mean you can actually get him up there on the stand?"

"You bet. We have already subpoenaed him."

"That should be interesting. Maybe I *will* eat something." She dipped her spoon into the broth.

"Mr. Kull," Quentin Thomas began. "By whom are you employed?"

The heavy-set man looked down at him from the witness stand. "Universal Patents."

"In what capacity?"

"President and Technical Director."

"Do your duties bring you into contact with the

computer-inventor that goes by the name of Faust?"

"Yes."

"In what way?"

"Well, among other things, I supervise Faust's utilization, maintenance, and repair."

"Looking simply at utilization, please explain just what that entails."

"I select the technical literature that he reads. Faust keeps current with about forty broad fields of technology: chemistry, electronics, mining, metallurgy, space vehicles, and so on. We subscribe to all the serious technical journals in these fields."

"You abstract these for him?"

"Oh, no. He reads them directly. We feed it into the slot. *Zot! Flip, flip, flip.* Every line, every page. All languages."

"And then what?"

"Then he invents. Based on the total technology in his data banks, he invents."

"Several inventions a day?"

Kull laughed. "Mr. Thomas, he cranks out about one thousand inventions a day!"

"So many? But not all of those are filed in the Patent Office?"

"No. He screens the gross output. He selects those of greatest value to society and industry. If a given invention looks as though it will be of reasonable value, he files it in the Patent Office."

"How many is that?"

"It averages about one hundred a day."

"What is the filing fee charged by the Patent Office? How much per patent application?"

"One hundred dollars per application."

"So it costs you, your company, ten thousand dollars a day just for filing expenses?"

"Yes, sir."

"Over two million dollars a year?"

"Well over."

"But you get this back in your licensing programs?"

"We do."

"You have heard testimony of the Commissioner of Patents to the effect that Morrissey—or Faust—or Universal Patents for the past several years has filed over ninety percent of the patent applications that are filed in the United States and in other industrial countries. Are licenses available under all of these patents?"

"They are indeed."

"By reason of this proliferation of patents, has Universal Patents acquired control of any substantial sector of American industry?"

"Objection!" Ordway was on his feet and hitching up his green robe. "Irrelevant!"

"Overruled," Speyer said.

"We have a certain amount of control over certain limited areas," Kull admitted.

"Isn't it a fact, Mr. Kull, that your patent structure covers every significant innovation introduced in industry since Faust began to invent?"

"Every? I don't know about *every*."

"*Most* of the innovations?"

Ordway was up again. "Your Honor, I object. Universal Patent's contributions to American industry are not at issue here. Furthermore, the, ah, question calls for a quantifying answer, necessarily involving considerable speculation by the witness."

"Your Honor," Quentin Thomas said, "we are attempting to show that plaintiff is attempting to monopolize all basic industrial technology through its patent structure. This is a concerted, long-enduring program that in itself constitutes an unreasonable restraint of trade, thereby violating the Sherman Antitrust Act. It is part of defendant's defense that even if the patent is valid and infringed, it is unenforceable for reasons of public policy. Plaintiff should not be permitted to kill this woman in pursuit of its technological stranglehold on the United States and indeed on the whole word!"

"I object to the inflammatory language, Your Honor," Ordway said harshly. "And I offer a continuing objection to testimony tending to show plaintiff's ownership of technology other than that in issue here. Such testimony is simply irrelevent."

"I will sustain your objection to Mr. Thomas's last question," Speyer ruled. He addressed defense counsel. "Now then, Mr. Thomas, please put the world conspiracy out of your mind. Move on to something more relevant."

Thomas turned back to the witness. "Mr. Kull, do your prospective licensees in industry ever resist your licensing terms?"

"Your client is resisting right now, Mr. Thomas."

A wave of nervous laughter floated over the audience. Speyer banged away with his gavel. "Please continue, Mr. Thomas."

"Have you ever taken over a licensee who could not pay your terms?"

"Objection!" Ordway roared.

"Sustained," Speyer said. "I must caution you, Mr. Thomas, I will not have this trial turned into an ad hominem attack against the patentee."

"Of course not, Your Honor. As a matter of fact, I express the greatest admiration for the patentee, Mr. Robert Morrissey." He turned back to the witness. "Mr. Kull, why is Mr. Morrissey not present here today?"

"Because he is presently confined to a sanitarium for the mentally ill. He is incompetent."

"And yet he files one hundred patent applications a day?"

"Yes."

"His mental condition does not seem to affect his inventive abilities?"

"Well, Mr. Thomas, I think you know the story there. He invented Faust and then he became insane. The inventive capacity of his computer-inventor was brought into being before he had his very lamentable mental lapse.

"Has a legal guardian been appointed for him?"

"Yes, sir."

"Who?"

"Myself."

"Who gets the money from the patents?"

"Well, of course, it's put in trust for Mr. Morrissey."

"Who is the trustee?"

"Universal Patents."

"Is there an instrument setting up the trust?"

"Objection!" Ordway said.

"Sustained," Speyer ruled. "Mr. Thomas, income from other patents has nothing to do with infringement or validity of the fiber patent. This whole line of inquiry is irrelevant. You are wasting the court's time."

He would have to come in from another direction. "Mr. Kull, is it your testimony that Faust simply looks at the literature and then comes up with his ideas?"

"Some of his inventions are made that way. For others, he conducts experiments."

"In a laboratory?"

"In a sense, yes. Faust carries within himself several laboratories."

"Chemical? Electronic?"

"Both. Faust contains a tiny chemical laboratory within his shell, with all standard pieces of laboratory equipment and analytical machinery, plus several hundred thousand chemical reagents. His chemical inventions are always tested in his laboratory before he files a patent application. And since he requires only a few hundred molecules to make a test, each test takes only a microsecond. Faust can conduct a chemical research program in ten minutes that would require several years for a conventional corporate laboratory."

"Does he contain anything else, Mr. Kull?"

"Faust has a tiny electric smelter, plus a stock of thousands of different metals and alloys. He has a permutative electronic circuit board capable of an almost infinite variety of circuits. He makes his own paper from the air: It is carbon dioxide based, of course. And he has a small nuclear reactor, plus some other things."

"And you contend, Mr. Kull, that all this work, these

experiments, these ideas, all of these are the inventions of a man in a mental institution?"

"Yes, sir. For Mr. Morrissey built Faust."

This was getting him nowhere. He had to try something else. "Mr. Kull, you heard Mr. Flagman's testimony to the effect that Faust filed about twenty thousand patent applications in the United States Patent Office last year. Do you recall that?"

"Yes, it was about twenty thousand."

"But we don't have a figure for this year. Say, for the first six months. Can you provide that."

Kull hesitated. Quentin Thomas noted that the big man suddenly looked uncomfortable. Aha, he thought. Possibilities at last?

"He filed about five thousand," Kull replied.

But that, Thomas thought, was the quota for only one quarter. Say February, March, and April? His heart leaped. That was it! "When did Faust stop filing?" he said quietly.

Kull shifted in the witness chair and looked over to Ordway as though for guidance. But Ordway seemed to have his eyes fixed on his papers. Kull said finally, "I don't recall exactly."

"Perhaps not exactly. But isn't it true that Faust did not file anything in the month of June?"

"Yes, I guess so."

"Nor in May? And very few, if any, in April?"

"That is correct."

"Why not, Mr. Kull. Did you turn him off?"

"No, we didn't turn him off."

"Did Faust explain his inactivity to you?"

"In a way."

"What did he say?"

"It doesn't make any sense."

"Let the jury be the judge of that. What did he say?"

"Faust claims he is through inventing in the field of industrial technology. He claims he is going on to other things."

"What other things?"

"Five things," Kull said tautly.

"Please name them, Mr. Kull."

"Well, first, the cure of certain diseases. Second, changing the size of objects. Third, transport of objects. Fourth, projection of the future into the present. Fifth, telekinetic control of certain chemical reactions."

Quentin Thomas had to pause and digest this. Was Kull serious? The U.P. president and technical director seemed deadly serious, and somewhat chagrined at having to reveal the shortcomings of the computer-inventor in open court. Thomas said, "Has Faust demonstrated any of these new projects?"

"No, of course not. I told you it wouldn't make any sense."

"I have nothing further," Thomas said.

"Cross, Mr. Ordway?" Speyer asked.

"No, Your Honor."

"You may stand down, Mr. Kull," Speyer said. "And I think we may as well recess for the weekend."

"Your Honor," Thomas said.

"Yes?" Speyer responded impatiently.

"Just one further matter, Your Honor. Defendant would like to have Mr. Robert Morrissey testify, if he can be found. We assume that Mr. Kull, as his guardian, knows where he is. Mr. Kull is in the courtroom just now, and I will ask the court to order Mr. Kull to produce Mr. Morrissey."

Ordway frowned. "Your Honor, it is my understanding that Mr. Morrissey is not only insane, he is gravely ill of a heart condition. It might be fatal to move him. Isn't that right, Mr. Kull?"

Kull looked mildly surprised but recovered quickly. "Heart condition? Yes, that's right. It would be very risky to move him."

Speyer thought about that. He spoke to Kull. "Do you in fact know the whereabouts of Mr. Morrissey?"

"Yes, Your Honor."

"And he is in fact so ill that he cannot be moved?"

"So I understand, Your Honor."

"Then bring a medical certificate to that effect.

Otherwise I shall expect you to produce Mr. Morrissey."

"Yes, Your Honor."

Later, Quentin Thomas and Ellen Welles stood outside under the courthouse portico and watched Kull and Ordway in heated discussion at the curb. Finally the two men entered separate vehicles and were absorbed into traffic. Kull and Ordway both know Robert Morrissey is completely sane and completely healthy, Quentin Thomas mused. Heart condition? Ha! But with all the money and power of Universal Patents behind them, they can probably find fifty doctors to sign that medical certificate. He grimaced. He didn't know whether to be disgusted or amused. "Let's go get something to eat," he said to Ellen Welles.

15

THE VENETIAN COURT

"You haven't asked how we did this afternoon," Thomas said.

It was eight in the evening and they were dawdling over coffee in a cheap but convenient restaurant near the courthouse.

"No," Ellen Welles said. "How did we do?"

"Not so good."

She did not press him.

"It's the new patent statute and the case law that has developed around it," he said. "There's been nothing like it since the Middle Ages. The Medicis and Borgias would feel right at home at a modern patent infringement trial."

"Did they have patents in those days?"

"Oh, sure. Of course, their patents were more in the nature of trade monopolies. They did not necessarily involve inventions. That came later. But in Florence, in 1450, the town council might give a favored merchant a patent on making gunpowder, or candles, or velvet. And if anybody else tried to make candles in

Florence, he would be in violation of the patent. This was a crime, and he could be executed for it. In Florence, the standard penalty for patent infringement was garroting. Milan used execution by musket, and the bore of the musket was different, depending on whether the patent infringer was Christian, Jew, or Muslim. In Rome, they loved to hang you. In Genoa, they chopped your head off."

"And in Venice?" she asked.

He suddenly regretted bringing up the comparision. Somehow he had trapped himself. "Poison," he said gravely. "In Venice, they made the infringer drink poison."

She swallowed hard, then smiled crookedly. "Times haven't changed much, have they?" He didn't answer. She frowned and spoke again, almost as though she were talking to herself. "It seems that everything we do—or don't do—is forcing us deeper into some kind of judicial trap. That the more innocent I am, the worse it will be for me." Her voice rose half an octave. "Is the entire legal system of this entire country haywire? Can't anything be done about Ordway and that bastard on the bench?"

"Calm down, Ellen."

"It isn't right."

"No, it isn't."

Her mouth twisted. "Someday, somehow, those people will get theirs."

He smiled wanly. That wasn't going to happen. Even if it did, she'd be long dead and would take no comfort in it. How to explain this to her? Perhaps he could lead in with a few pompous generalities. "Sometimes it is left to history to vindicate the unjustly accused," he said carefully. "Their contemporaries tend to reward—not punish—the erring judge and prosecutor. Pontius Pilate served out his term as procurator and returned to Rome and the emperor's congratulations. And did you know the Abyssinian Church canonized him? Pierre Cauchon burned Joan of Arc and was promoted to Bishop of Lisieux. Elizabeth I beheaded Mary, Queen of Scots, and became England's most beloved sovereign since King Arthur. General Mercier, who helped frame Alfred Dreyfus to save the honor of the French Army, got a nice promotion out of it. And in more recent times, after he refused to pardon Sacco and Vanzetti, Governor Fuller of Massachusetts found himself a serious contender for the Republican vice-presidential nomination and was also mentioned as a good possibility as ambassador to France. We might as well be realistic, Ellen."

"So what will happen to Speyer?"

The lawyer shrugged. "He'll probably make it to the circuit court of appeals. Very prestigious, good money, immense power. The power's the main thing, of course." He helped her from the table, and they made their way to the cashier. Outside, the sky was dark and overcast. He put her in a cab and bade her good night. "Try to relax and rest," he admonished. "Get ready for Monday." Because Monday, you die, he couldn't help thinking.

She essayed a half smile. It didn't work.

He watched the cab move away, and his thoughts returned to Ordway and Kull. Barely an hour ago, those denizens of the legal half-world had stood on that very spot, arguing in low voices, and then they had gone their separate ways. Thomas was especially interested in Kull. What weekend destiny had called the master machinator? Certainly something with an important bearing on the litigation. But *what?* Or perhaps, *who?* Was Kull off to pay a mysterious midnight visit to someone? And if so, to whom? Whom did Kull need at this stage? Nobody. Kull had the case won. But maybe Kull wasn't as certain about that as counsel for the defense. Maybe Kull was out for extra insurance, to increase his chances from ninety-five percent up to a full one hundred persent. How? Not by bringing *in* a witness. Quite the contrary. Kull was going to *exclude* a witness.

He pulled out his pocket com. "Legal Data."

"Yes, Mr. Thomas?"

"Mr. Jethro Kull left the Federal Building an hour and a half ago. He got into a car at the curb. Where is he now?"

"We cannot trace a private car, Mr. Thomas. No information. No charge."

Thomas frowned and returned the com to his jacket pocket. He wasn't asking the right questions. But what *were* the right questions? He walked back to his apartment deep in thought.

16

SPEYER AND FRIENDS

Judge Speyer, tweezers in hand, was addressing a friend in the privacy of his bachelor lodgings. His voice was more musing than informative, more introspective than demanding.

"My dear, did you ever stop to wonder why I wanted to become a federal judge? You didn't. Well, I can tell you. It was the immense power, the incredible control to be wielded over human destinies. It would make up for the school years, when I had been pushed around by bigger boys, and later of being lost in the lower echelons of city politics, and still later when I became an assistant D.A. and was assigned all the drug cases."

He paused for a moment of contemplation. His audience listened to all this without apparent comprehension or response. She simply stared back at him with brilliant black eyes.

It is early morning. He sits motionless in the alley, on that little camp stool, behind the bookstore, looking down toward the restaurant. Cradled in his lap is the Mossberg laser with telescopic sights and silencer. It is set on 0.2—just enough to paralyze. Five or six garbage cans sit behind the restaurant. No covers. Perfect for rats. Sometimes as many as twenty. Hard to keep accurate count. They merge, blend. A writhing furry carpet. And here they are. Two big ones to start. In the same can. He raises the weapon. Lines up number one in the cross hairs. A sharp sigh as he squeezes the trigger. The quarry jumps, falls back, quivering a little. His pulses pound. Next, and next, and next. God, this is wonderful. Con Law final this this morning at eight-thirty. Three-hour exam. The way I'm getting charged up, I'm good for all day. Now they're beginning to eat each other. Damn! Watch the blood spurt! Like a shark feeding-frenzy. Wow! Always leave some to eat the ones you knock out. What's the right ratio of shot to unshot? The inspiration of hot, freshly spilled blood. Frederick Nietzsche understood this. It was something necessary for the accomplishment of great things. The great Turk Omar, at the gates of Byzantium that morning in 1453. Took his sword, slew his mistress as she knelt there pleading. Cleaved her, from skull to crotch. And then he led his janissaries off to the final, successful assault that changed history.

Years ago, way back in G. W. Law School. Whenever he had an important exam, he'd get the Mossberg out. It had carried him through school and through the D.C. bar exams. Rats went back even farther than that. Biology major. Thesis in his senior year. Effect of HCN on Rats. Determination of LD-50 dosage that would kill half the sample. Effect of HCN on organs of the survivors. Loved to guillotine them in the auto chopper. This was called "sacrificing." After a session he was able to write for forty-eight hours straight. Day and night. A plus on his HCN thesis, and it was deserved.

*   *   *

Somewhere in the middle of his senior year in law school he had been caught. By old Schmidt, assistant dean, no less. Schmidt, the early-morning jogger. Schmidt of the wise, hard eyes, the deviled-up eyebrows. "Speyer, come around to my office in the morning." And so young Rex Speyer had duly and fearfully appeared. Schmidt was leaning back in that thick-padded swivel chair, like a judge, with his soft leather shoes propped up on his desk. Speyer's dossier was spread out over a helter skelter of texts and exam papers. "You pulled seven ninety-nine on your LSAT," the dean said thoughtfully. "That's out of a possible eight hundred. Highest I've ever seen. Possibly the highest in history. And you're an A plus here: a straight four point oh. If somebody doesn't kill you first, you should expect to graduate as high man in your class. On the other hand"—the dean took his feet down and leaned forward—"Speyer, you are one sick shit."

Cold fear. "Does that mean I'm expelled?"

"Oh, hell, no. It just means you need therapy. You'll have to see Doc Stein, our resident psychiatrist. I've already made an appointment for you. Also, looking at your problem, long term, I think you ought not to go in with a firm. You shouldn't try to represent a client. You can't count on killing rats the morning before you appear in court. You'll have to get into some other branch of the law."

"Like what?"

Schmidt grinned at him. "Start with assistant D.A. After that, try for a judgeship. The bench is loaded with psychos. You won't be noticed. Do any damn thing you want, almost. Immense power. You want to kill somebody? Get the circuit to assign the murder cases to you. A truly effective judge can force a jury to find Jesus Christ guilty of killing Pontius Pilate. Sentence a man to the chair, young fellow, and you'll float around for a week."

And the old bastard had been right. Funny how it had all worked out. He had indeed graduated. He and

three hundred other aspirants. He remembered that
night, in Constitution Hall. The incredibly dull
speeches. The vice president of the United States had
been granted a juris doctor degree, honoris causa. His
speech was the most dull of all. And then the line
formed to walk up on the platform, where the dean
handed him the roll of synparchment tied with the
gold ribbon.

His name was called. "Rex Whitney Speyer!" And
he walked over and picked up the hunting license for
his forthcoming legal career.

Rex Whitney Speyer.

His father had died when he was an infant, and he
had no recollection of him. He liked his surname. It
had a satisfactory teutonic sibilance. He didn't like
Whitney. That was his mother's family. *Rex* he hated.
She had named him that. Rex meant king, and it had
been a continuing source of trouble and humiliation.

The night before he graduated from law school he
and a half dozen of his fellow graduates had gone
over to that place in Georgetown. It was the annual
custom, and the girls there knew they were entertain-
ing law graduates. This girl, younger even than he,
took him upstairs to her room. She had been thin,
with high cheekbones and dark hair, almost black.
And a look of bright intelligence. She could have sat
next to him in Future Interests and looked right at
home. Did she remind him of someone? Yes, she did.
And right then and there, in her room, he realized
who. His mother. Of course. And then it was all
useless. He couldn't do anything. But worse was to
come. She studied the situation a moment, then she
laughed at him. Not in scorn. The bitch laughed in
sheer merriment, and then she quoted that damn
limerick. Not even knowing his name, she fed it to him:

> There was a young fellow named Rex
> Who had minuscule organs of sex.
> When arraigned for exposure

He replied with composure,
"De minimis non curat lex."

There was a simpler name for it: castration. His
mother had done that to him.

Anybody can be a judge, Dean Schmidt had said.
Just a question of politics, of knowing somebody. Or
money. Enough money would make up for almost any
kind of deficiency. There were about nineteen thousand judges in state and local courts; about four
hundred twenty-five in federal trial courts; about one
hundred in the federal courts of appeal. And finally,
nine—just nine—in the U.S. Supreme Court. Where
to start? He would get some money, then get himself
a federal judgeship.

Why would anyone want to be a federal judge? It
wasn't the peanut-salary: fifty thousand a year, plus
fringe benefits. A good lawyer with a metropolitan
practice could clear five times that. Well, then what
was it? It was the authority, the power, the near
omnipotence, the ability to control people's lives. And
it was a lifetime job. He could be fired only for
"treason, or other high crimes and misdemeanors."
His personal quirks were irrelevant. He had personal,
arbitrary, capricious power unequaled since the kings
of France. Oh, it got him in the gut. A wonderful,
wonderful feeling.

"Are you attending, my dear?" he said to his un-
responsive listener. "It all began to happen when my
mother died." He paused a moment, as if to think
about that. He shook the tweezers viciously as he
returned to his explanation. "I knew instantly what
I was going to do with the inheritance: with one half of
it, I would buy a federal judgeship, the very next one
that fell vacant in my home state. And so I contributed
generously to Senator Wilford Berwin's reelection
campaign, and the senator put my name up before the
Senate Judiciary Committee. The FBI made its routine
investigation into my past and found nothing. The

American Bar Association researched my legal accomplishments." He paused and frowned. He just couldn't bring himself to say out loud what the A.B.A. had done to him.

The A.B.A. had four categories: exceptionally well qualified, well qualified, qualified, and not qualified. And they had reported him as "not qualified." He knew the definition well. "A person so classified has been found unsatisfactory as to either professional ability, experience, temperament, or integrity."

He had been able to get a copy of the report from the confidential files of the A.B.A. It still hurt to think about some of the language they had used. "A sick man. Not to be trusted with life-and-death courtroom decisions." The A.B.A. psychoprofiler had even visited his psychiatrist, who, however, refused to be interviewed, very properly claiming patient-physician privilege. But no matter—he had never gone back to the foolish man. Why? Because Stein was an errant liar. Or at least his electronics lied; the truth was not in them. That sorry jumble of wires and microchips wouldn't last a minute in *his* court. Well, that time under hypnosis. Stein had taken him back . . .

Back . . . he was, what?—ten years old. And he had done something he couldn't really remember exactly. Think . . . he knew . . . Yes, he had watched his mother leave her bath without her robe. . . . She was nude. . . . He had hidden where he could do this, and he had waited . . . he had seen her beautiful body . . . everything . . . and he knew it was wrong to see her . . . he had tried to run . . . and *she* had seen *him*. After she dressed she found him, cowering in his toy closet, and she had tied him up with his cowboy lariat—miles and miles of it—arms and legs immobile. . . . "No, Momma! Please, Momma!" Draining away to a wail.

Except, of course, it was all electronic fantasy. He would have remembered anything that important.

Stein had been partly right on other matters, at
least. Speyer gave him that. "Somehow reminds me of
the great Harry Stack Sullivan," said Dr. Stein. "Marvelous practitioner. Wrote on interpersonal relations.
Harry had these recurring nightmares about a giant
spider. He worked it out—catharsized it, if you will—
where he identified the spider with his mother's geni-
talia. Oedipus to Jocasta: You've got a spider—*there*,
you bitch! Weird, eh? He was fighting a subconscious
incest motif, of course. Well, once he nailed it down,
the nightmares stopped."

"To hell with Harry what's his name. And keep my
mother out of this."

"She's *in* it, don't you see? But the point I'm making
is, you did your undergraduate work in biology. And
you need a hobby. Raise spiders!"

Dr. Argos Stein, the seeing stone. In general, a
totally messed-up kook. But that one time he had
been right. Spiders turned out to be a marvelous
hobby. He had got out all the books. Fabre. He had
brought the cages and terrariums into his apartment.
He became hooked on spiders.

But raising spiders did not catharsize anything. *There*
Stein had been wrong. Of course. There was nothing
to catharsize. He wasn't sick. It was as simple as that.
Stein was just wrong. And he, Speyer, finally decided
he liked himself just as he was. And that ended the
sessions. Maybe Stein was sick. Perhaps the world was
crazy. But Rex Speyer was neither.

He twisted the tweezers in the air toward his favorite.
"But to hell with the A.B.A." As it turned out, they
didn't matter at all. Not that he had forgotten them.
No, indeed. In fact, he had gotten the names of the
A.B.A. committee, and vowed that each and every
one of them would suffer if he ever had a case in *his*
court.

"And so, my delicate one," he continued, "the
President, at Berwin's insistent urging, duly nominated
me, and I duly appeared before the Senate Judiciary
Committee for my examination. But the money had

already been paid, and the questions were perfunctory. There were three senators, and each asked one question. I had been briefed on the questions, and I knew exactly how to reply.

Question: How do you feel about the death penalty?
Answer: I'm for it.
Question: And the Warren Court?
Answer: Perhaps a moot question. All decisions involving permissiveness have been overturned, and properly so. I intend to keep them that way.
Question: What do you think of Learned Hand?
Answer: A great judicial philosophy. Yet his recommendation that a criminal trial be conducted so as to let a guilty man go free rather than let an innocent man be hanged—*that's* clear error.

"And so the Senate duly confirmed me, and I ascended to the bench."

As he walked over to the fly cage he called back over his shoulder. "But do you think I intend to remain a federal judge forever? Hah! No, indeed, my beauty, I do *not* intend to stop here. There are two more steps upward I am determined to make. The first is to be appointed to a federal appellate court. Not that I really relish being a federal appellate judge. But I recognize that I will have to take *that* step in order to qualify for my second and final goal—the United States Supreme Court." He thought about that. "And I'll make a good Supreme Court justice. How will history regard me? Well, my dear, look at it this way.

"Fifty years ago a panel of sixty-five law professors, historians, and political scientists voted on the twelve greatest American jurists of all time: Holmes, Brandeis, Marshall, Story, Taney, John Marshall Harlan, Hughes, Harlan Stone, Cardozo, Black, Frankfurter, and Warren."

He looked across the room as though to make clear

a very simple fact of life. "No names have been added since that original poll. It's time to include another—*mine!*" Names in lights, emblazoned across the legal skies! Oliver Wendell Holmes. Rex Whitney Speyer. Louis Brandeis! "That'll be about where they'll fit me in." And if one name had to drop out to keep the roster to an even dozen, it would be Earl Warren. Of course.

He smiled and turned back to drop a conspiratorial comment. "It is said that a federal judge is a lawyer who knew a senator, and that a Supreme Court justice is a judge who knew a President. Well, I know the President, and if I don't get appointed by this one, then I will certainly take pains to become known to the next one!"

His brow wrinkled, as though he had almost overlooked a salient point. "All of this," he admitted, "is founded on the proposition that I can turn out a milestone opinion in that damned antitrust case. But, in order to get sufficiently charged up to write *that* one, I first have to get psyched up on this weird patent case. Anyone with legs as gorgeous as yours can surely understand that." He nodded, as though to answer for her. "And now it's all falling into place. That woman will die Monday afternoon. Monday evening I will start dictating the antitrust opinion. Articles on my opinion will start coming out in the law journals in four to six months. They'll compare me to Learned Hand, of New York; to Traynor, of California. Within the year, I'll have a fair shot at the next appellate vacancy. In another four or five years, the Supreme Court. It's there. It's within our grasp. And the money's there."

He considered his finances. He had spent a lot, both on his career and on things he considered essentials. But there was plenty left. Over four million. He considered some of those essentials.

A fair portion of his inheritance had gone into locating one of the few remaining originals of that fantastic morality play, *Mystère de la Passion,* written by Gilles de Laval Retz in the early fifteenth century. The famous—some said infamous—marshal of France, patron of literature and music, skilled illuminator and binder, had composed the *Mystère* while inspired by the torture-murder of a few local peasant boys. One hundred forty to one hundred fifty, some said. Irrelevant. Speyer was saddened when he thought about it. Oh, how history had misjudged the great de Retz! What were a few unknown sniveling wretches compared to the *Mystère?* But of course the unfeeling philistines of the day had created an uproar, and his hero, alas, had been hanged.

His gaze shifted to a gilt-framed engraved portrait, in profile. He noted with approval the high jacket collar, the hair gathered to the rear of the head in a single pigtail. It is a late eighteenth century head. The profiled eye was lustrous and gleaming, the sensuous mouth slightly parted, as though the mind was occupied in contemplation of some very attractive project. Ah yes, this was the mind that created *Justine, Juliette, The Crimes of Love,* and all those other marvelous fantasies. The remarkable thing was that the creation took place within the confines of the Bastille, where the owner of that mind had been placed because of certain, well, lack of appreciation of certain oddities in the monolithic minds of the Paris police. But the memories and mental repetition of those oddities must indeed have been the inspiration for the literature this man cranked out during his prison sojourn. So strange that he, Speyer, a simple American jurist, was probably one of the few who really understood that great man, who had given his name to a certain kind of behavior.

He saluted the portrait with the tweezers. "Here's to you, Donatien Alphonse Francois, Marquis de Sade."

He reached the fly cage. With a quick deft movement he snatched out one of its occupants with the tweezers and retraced his steps to the terrarium. "You should see her, dearest Atropos. Perhaps Monday I shall bring you her picture. I can assure you, with that hood and dressed in black, she looks very much like a fly. Speaking of which, madame—"

The judge slipped the protesting fly through the feeding hole of the screened cage. Its first frantic circuit of the enclosure hurled it into the waiting web. Atropos, from her sentry post in the center of the web, instantly sensed the nature of her supper from the microcurrents set up in the radial filaments. She ran across the reticules in a flash and began wrapping her protesting guest in an imprisoning silken jacket. When that was done, she bit the fly in the head and began to suck the juices from the dying creature. The blue and red bands on her abdomen pumped in slow pleasured rhythm.

Judge Speyer watched in fascination.

From the dozens of screened cages set on the shelves in his study arose a susurrus, a minute multiplied rustling of impatient mandibles. A contented smile wreathed the judge's flaccid features. "Ah, my children, I am coming." He walked over to the fly-breeding cage again. "Patience, my darlings. There is enough for all."

17

MOIRA WHITNEY SPEYER

Background. Quentin Thomas needed to know more about Speyer. He studied the printout of the judge's bio. He didn't really know what he was looking for, but thought he might recognize it if he saw it.

What was important? What could be skipped? "Unresolved Oedipal conflicts." What the hell did that mean? Something to do with the man's mother, of course. Start with her.

He punched in. "Legal Data."

"Here, Mr. Thomas."

"Biography of Mrs. Moira Whitney Speyer."

"One thousand dollars, Mr. Thomas."

"Accepted."

"Print, or oral?"

"Printout, please."

It was instantly on his screen. He read it quickly.

Moira Whitney Speyer, 1948–1998. Married Dale Speyer, 1968. One son, Rex Whitney Speyer, born 1970. Left estate $9,000,000.

Son sole heir. Lived in Lucerne, Switzerland, 1988 until death. Buried there.

Questions clamored at him. Did she and her son
see each other regularly? Check passport records,
visas, airline rosters. He punched in again, and the
scattered data began to flow in. The records showed
that she never left Switzerland. But how about *him*?
Didn't *he* visit *her*?

That one was easy. He very quickly determined that
Rex Speyer did not hold a passport; the judge had
probably never been overseas in his entire life.

But did they write each other? Exchange birthday
greetings? Christmas cards?

No record.

What did she die of?

Leukemia. Her condition did not respond to pro-
longed chemotherapy.

Didn't anyone tell him?

At the end, she tried to phone him. He would not
take the call.

What was her last attempt?

This:

Judge R. W. Speyer, Federal Court House
Port City, Maryland, U.S.A.

Your mother expected to die within forty eight
hours. She requests your presence.

> K. Atelon, Administrator
> Hôpital Bon Secours

His reply?

No reply of record.

The answer was pounding, pounding at him. "I want
a holo of Mrs. Speyer," he said grimly.

The scene shown him was of a little figure on a city
street. He couldn't see her face. Her dress and hat
identified her as a woman of conservative tastes, but
aside from that she could have been anyone.

"Lucerne?" he muttered, disappointed.

"Yes. The most recent. Her last time out, before becoming bedridden."

"Not good enough. Something earlier, and showing her face. Say, when she was thirty-five to forty years old."

The next one seemed to be some kind of garden party. Lots of people, men and women, holding drinks. He could even imagine a muted chatter. Down the white pebbled path came a woman. He knew it was going to be *she*, Moria Whitney Speyer. He turned up the magnification. She faced the holo cameras. She was mugging, really. First, that marvelous profile, then the cold, beautiful, three-quarter face. There was something about the high checkbones, the astral beauty of the sunken eyes.

It pole-axed him. *That* face was almost indistinguishable from the face of Ellen Welles. Judge Rex Whitney Speyer was going to avenge a lifetime of neglect and maternal contempt. Among his other subterranean motivations, the judge would include a touch of socially acceptable matricide.

Thomas had been through murder trials, but he had never encountered anything like this. He had a sensation of drowning. Every time he tried to take a breath he seemed to gulp down a lungful of horror.

Ironically, understanding this didn't really help. To know why Speyer was determined to kill Ellen Welles did nothing to save her life. Quite the contrary; it left him almost paralyzed.

He had to get hold of himself.

"Turn it off," he whispered. The scene faded.

He stared into nothing for a long time. Then he got up and headed for the bedroom. It had been a long day. He needed some sleep.

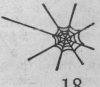

18

A VIEW OF
THE MOUNTAINS

Later that night Quentin Thomas paced the rooms of his suite, his hands folded behind his back. He had to find Morrissey and get him on the stand. And fast. He had the weekend to do this. Saturday and Sunday. But even Legal Data didn't know Morrissey's whereabouts. Kull knew. Ordway knew. But certainly *they* weren't going to bring in Morrissey. They would bring in a phony document certifying that the great inventor couldn't be moved.

That left Faust. Did Faust know? Would Faust urge that his creator be found yet not provide instructions for finding him?

He was missing something. Somewhere hidden away in that mass of educational games and oddities designed by Faust were other clues. A road map? An "X" marks the spot"? A simple statement? No, Faust would not risk detection by anything so blatant. Universal Patents would be watching for something like that, and when they saw it they'd simply withdraw the product from the market. No, it would be subtler. Much subtler.

But where to start? He'd have to relax, and let his mind wander; perhaps then he'd think of something. He walked into his art room, sat down in front of the "canvas," placed the cranial cap on his head, and began the initial relaxation process. He was quite wound up, and it was a good five minutes before he tried his imagination. He had done it many times, yet he never ceased to marvel. He was mind-painting. First, he would think of a picture, say Van Gogh's *The Road to Arles*. The cap would pick up the minute alpha, beta, and gamma waves from the cerebral cortex. These would be decoded, run through a line scanner, and translated into electrical impulses that impinged on the prepared canvas. The canvas was coated with millions of color clusters, tiny dots consisting of even smaller subdots of colored resin: blue, yellow, red, plus black and white, at first hidden under a concealing layer of lacquer. The impulse from his brain would pick one of these subdots and dwell on it long enough to melt its lacquer cover, thereby bringing it to the surface of the canvas. When joined by a few million of its fellows, the whole made an image, in color.

And now, what would he mind-paint? He let his thoughts wander freely. He pondered the events of this first day of the trial, but the courtroom faded, the faces of the actors becoming blurred, indistinct. He picked up a scene or two from his childhood. The front of the YMCA, where he had gone swimming. Was this what he was looking for? No, he would not punch in the recorder yet. Keep going. Another building appeared. It was white brick, too. He closed his eyes and relaxed totally. He did not recognize the structure. Interesting. In the background stretched a low mountain ridge. His heart began to beat faster, for here was something he *did* recognize. In this scene the sun was setting, and its last beams lit up the crags in the center of his panorama. He knew those rocks. It was the face of Stony Man, a cliff formation in the Shenandoah National Park, in northern Virginia. He had climbed the path to Stony Man many a time in his youth. The building that his mind-painting set wanted him to see was in the Shenandoah Valley, not too far from Washington, D.C. He could pretty well pinpoint the location. But why should he have any interest whatever in this building?

He let his mind wander back to the white brick front. The building had two stories, and it looked peaceful enough. Green lawn in front, flower beds. All well cared for. White pebble driveway circling up to the main drive and out again.

Then the peculiarities began to jump out at him. There was a sign at the entrance to the driveway: "No Trespassing." A closer inspection of the windows revealed that they were laced with bars. And on the bars were rectangles of electrical tape. Why? To keep someone in? To keep the public out?

He now noticed, for the first time, another oddity, in the lower righthand corner of the canvas: "Copyright, 2008, Universal Patents." Of course! Heart pounding, he pressed the "print" button. The image was instantly fixed on the panel. He felt like slapping his forehead. The solution to Morrissey's whereabouts had been staring him in the face all these months. Another message from Faust.

He was actually going to get away to the mountains for a few hours! And right in the middle of a case!

He ripped off the cranial cap and jumped to his feet. It was now into the early hours of Saturday morning. He hadn't a moment to lose. He ran over to the intercom and called the penthouse garage. "Eddie!"

A sleepy voice answered. "Yes, sir, Mr. Thomas?"

"Get the Chameleon out. I'm on my way to the elevator right now."

"Yeah, okay, Mr. Thomas."

The little craft was waiting for him when he stepped out on the roof. He pulled the antimeddler from his inner jacket pocket. He unwound the little cable and plugged the tip into the adapter socket in the side of the Chamelon, just over the door. Immediately the little red light on the device began to flash.

So U.P. had gotten to his little craft. Dirty pool. Innocent people—including himself—might have been killed.

He unfolded the analysis plate in the antimeddler and began the search. Engine block. Ignition. Gearing. Repulsors. Frame. Outer skin. Seats and internal furnishings. Landing assembly. Flash. Flash. Flash. He backed up. Wheel supports. Nothing. Right wheel. Left wheel. Flash. Flash. Flash.

He knelt down. The left wheel was *wrong*. It was brand new. He touched it tentatively. The polyolefin skin felt funny. It had a rough, almost abrasive quality to it. The whole wheel probably was hardened plastic explosive. And how detonated?

He found it: a microaltimeter plus detonator cap. With gauge, no less! Set for three hundred meters, normal altitude for city traffic.

He had no time to get this thing off and put another wheel on. He thought a moment, then took out a ballpoint pen and very carefully touched the index on the little altimeter. Nothing happened. He started moving the indicator to the right. Three hundred fifty. Four hundred. Five. Six. One thousand. Two thousand. Five. How high was Mount Everest? He moved the indicator to ten thousand meters.

Was that all there was to it? Somehow he thought he would have been easier to kill.

He had followed the routine before, but this was his first alert. He owed his life to the makers of the little gimmick, and he didn't even know whom to thank. He turned the antimeddler over and looked at the manufacturer's tag: Made under license from Universal Patents. His mouth contorted into a harsh grin. It was the penalty of size. U.P. was so big, so sprawling, their right hand didn't know what their left hand was doing.

He got into the cabin, slammed the door behind him, and turned on the antigravs. He punched in the coordinates for the Shenandoah route, and the little ship sailed along through the night.

He had to get organized. If Robert Morrissey was really being held prisoner in that white brick building, who might be with him tonight? Kull, of course. That was why Kull and Ordway had gone their separate ways. That was why Kull and Ordway were having that very serious discussion at the streetside, just after the trial ended yesterday. They were deciding what to do with Robert Morrissey. Were they going to have him killed?

What he had been trying to come to terms with ever since he had agreed to take the Welles case now struck him—the enormous scope and power of Universal Patents. They truly did have the industrial world in the palms of their hands. Hundreds of billions of dollars were at stake. They would think nothing of a murder or two. It was a wonder that Robert Morrissey had lived so long, if indeed he was still alive!

As soon as he was out of metropolitan traffic he got on the communicator. "Legal Data."

"Legal Data here, Mr. Thomas."

"Daniel Ordway, O-R-D-W-A-Y, general counsel for Universal Patents, has a secret scrambler line. How much?"

"Ordway, representing U.P. in *U.P.* v. *Welles*?"

Thomas sighed. The price had just doubled. "Yes."

"Three hundred thousand dollars."

"Too high."

"Mr. Thomas, you must realize giving you this information is a prison offense." The voice held a plaintive edge. "Our contacts in the phone company have just raised *their* fees. We have to pass the expense along if we are going to stay in business. And then there's overhead, our escrow for legal fees if we are caught, plus taxes. These are inflationary times, Mr. Thomas."

"A month ago it was a hundred and fifty thousand."

"And now it is three hundred thousand. Take it or leave it, Mr. Thomas."

"Throw in Ordway's voice overlay, and I will take it."

"Ah, so you are going to impersonate Mr. Ordway on his own secret scrambler? The voice overlay will be an extra twenty-five thousand. Total, three hundred twenty-five thousand, Mr. Thomas."

He groaned. "It's a deal. Three twenty-five."

"Cash in advance, as usual."

"Of course," Thomas said grimly. "Here's the access." He punched in the credit transfer.

"The scrambled index is 5316189," the voice told him. "Is your modifier open?"

"It's open."

"Fine. Here's Ordway's voice overlay. Just watch for those spaced intervals. Like he's always arguing a case in court. This'll make you a perfect imitation. Very convincing. End of transmission. Got it, Mr. Thomas?"

"Got it." As he punched out, he pondered Legal Data with mingled bitterness, envy, gratitude, and awe. Legal Data: all kinds of services for all kinds of lawyers. And at all prices. Legal Data could duplicate keys to safe-deposit boxes overnight. They could produce the combination to any safe in the country within forty-eight hours. They forged passports, driver's licenses, and vehicle titles. They knew the balance in your checking account. They engineered child custody kidnappings. Lawyers had been disbarred for simply calling them for a weather report.

But there was one thing even Legal Data didn't know, unless they had picked it up within the last few hours. He came back to the communicator. "Legal Data?"

"Yes, Mr. Thomas."

"Do you know the whereabouts of Robert Morrissey?"

"No, we still don't know. Do you want to be notified if we find out?"

"No, not yet, anyway." He punched out; at the same moment his traffic receptor began to beep.

He punched in. "Yes?"

"QT/701?"

"Yes, here."

"This is Shenandoah Traffic Control. We warn you to watch for an antigrav van about three kilometers ahead of you, on your identical flight pattern. Do you see on your screen?"

"Yes. It is just now coming in over the edge."

"The other craft is leveling at five thousand meters," the voice continued in a monotone. "Since you are the faster, we are ascending you to seventy-five hundred. Please acknowledge."

"Acknowledged. Is that a commercial craft?"

"We cannot give you further information. Out."

This was ominous. He had to know. "Legal Data."

"Here, Mr. Thomas."

"I have a craft preceding me in my line of flight. It is headed for a touchdown in the Shenandoah Valley, just west of the little town of Luray, Virginia. What cargo?"

There was a pause. "Twenty-five thousand dollars, Mr. Thomas."

He hid his surprise. Legal Data broke in, "You were perhaps wondering, why so cheap?"

"The thought occurred to me."

"It's because we can't guarantee cargo identity. It is at best a probability. Do you still want it?"

"Yes. Here's the credit transfer."

"It's a commercial antigrav van, as you probably know. It last stopped at Earth Excavators, Inc., in Jessup, Maryland. It picked up something there, apparently not of any great size, plus one passenger, apparently an equipment operator."

He thought rapidly. An earth excavator, small enough to fit into an antigrav van. It would be only one thing—a gravedigger.

His throat tightened. "Legal Data?"

"Here, Mr. Thomas."

"I want you to feed a different set of destination coords to that van."

"You know we can't do that, Mr. Thomas. We

would have to have at least three contacts at Shenandoah Traffic Control. The cost would be exorbitant."

"I know for a fact you have at least one man there. He can set up the other two. The deviation will actually be very slight, to the next farmhouse down the road. A few seconds of arc. Undetectable. If there should ever be an investigation it will be charged to pilot error."

"What you are asking is against the law, Mr. Thomas. Interference with flight path is a federal offense. U..S Code, Section 1209. Ten years in prison."

"How much?"

"Five hundred thousand. Cash. Immediate transfer."

He gulped. This would just about wipe him out. "Here's the access. You have five minutes. If you can't deliver within that time, I want my money back."

"Fair enough, Mr. Thomas."

He punched out. Greedy bastards. But thank God they existed. He focused his attention on that bright dot on the radar screen. Was it veering off just the tiniest bit? So soon? How could that be? There were various possibilities. Perhaps Legal Data already had its necessary contacts at Shenandoah Traffic Control. Or perhaps they had bypassed Shenandoah Traffic altogether and made their deal directly with the van pilot. That would probably be quicker, cheaper, and would, of course, involve less risk. And finally, they might well have jammed the van's proper coords and substituted another set. That alternative would have been the cheapest possible variation, with the least risk. It would have required electronic wizardry of a high order, but it was quite possible that Legal Data had done it. He shrugged. The less he knew about it, the better.

It was time for the Chameleon to assume a different attire. He typed out the letters on his panel keyboard:

EARTH EXCAVATORS, INC.
JESSUP, MD.

He couldn't see outside, but if all was in working order, that legend now illuminated the sides of his little ship. He peered out through the darkness. The lights of Luray were coming up. It was time to contact Kull.

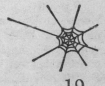

19

A PROPOSED INJECTION

"We have now come to the end of the line, Mr. Morrissey," Jethro Kull said. "The parting of the ways." He folded his arms across his chest. His black eyes glistened, and his mouth flattened into an implacable line.

Robert Morrissey looked through the barred windows toward the low-lying mountains, barely visible against the night sky, then back to his tormentor. His long uncut hair fell down past his shoulders. He pulled a strand away from his eyes and, as if in counterpoint to Kull, folded his arms behind his back.

Kull continued, almost defensively. "I have been fair, Morrissey, but you refused to cooperate. Without me, Faust would not exist. When you were building the computer, you were always short of money. You turned to me, and I put up the money you needed to finish Faust. You seem to have forgotten that."

"In return for your money I gave you one third of the prospective licensing proceeds. That was our deal. *You* seem to have forgotten *that*."

"I was entitled to more. *Much* more."

"So you said. When Faust began to operate, when he began turning out one invention after another, you became greedy. You wanted more. I wanted to license Faust's inventions to industry at nominal royalties. *You* wanted to use the patents to take over the economy."

"You were insane, Morrissey," Kull murmured. "You still are."

"So you got your crooked court order, and that lawyer Ordway and you had me committed, sent to my own private jail here in the mountains. You had yourself appointed my legal guardian, and then you and Ordway set up Universal Patents to take title to Faust's patents, in trust for me."

A hard smile twisted Kull's face. "All very true, and all very legal."

"One might think it would have been simpler to kill me."

The smile remained, but Kull was silent.

Morrissey continued. "You did not kill me because you encountered a small legal difficulty. I have no heirs. If you kill me, my two-thirds interest in Faust, Faust's patents, and all that licensing income would escheat to the State of Virginia."

"Quite so."

"And yet, even assuming you could force me to assign interest to Universal Patents, the assignment would not be valid, because I am insane, not competent to assign anything. And you, Kull, because you are my guardian, could not lawfully sell my two-thirds interest to your own corporation. No court would ratify such a phony deal."

"Very perceptive, Mr. Morrissey."

"And these little legal tangles have kept me alive."

Jethro Kull cocked his head. "Do you hear anything, Mr. Morrissey?"

The inventor looked out the window. In the distance they could hear a rhythmic beat. Morrissey shrugged his shoulders. "An antigrav. They fly over every once in a while."

Kull glanced at his watch. "This is a special van, Mr. Morrissey."

"Is this what you meant by 'a parting of the ways'? Are you moving me?"

"Well, in a sense, I suppose you could say that. Let's back up a bit, Mr. Morrissey. Your analysis of the legal situation was fairly accurate. You can't sign a valid bill of sale, because you are crazy. Nor can I, acting as your legal guardian, sell your interest in Faust to my own corporation, because the equity court would never ratify it. So, Morrissey, you force us into a slightly illegal undertaking, which, but for your persistent intransigence, we would never have contemplated."

Morrissey's face set in grim lines. "Go on."

Kull pulled a blue-backed document from his inner jacket pocket and handed it to the other man. "This is your copy, Morrissey. Ours is in the corporation safe."

The inventor read quickly. The document was titled "Bill of Sale." It was short and simple. By its terms, he, Robert Morrissey, assigned, transferred, and conveyed to Universal Patents all of his right, title, and interest in and to that computer device known as Faust; all past, present, and future work product of Faust, including patents; and all income resulting from said work product. He looked for his signature. "Good forgery," he mutttered.

"Done by the best penman in the East," Kull said. "We paid a lot for that."

"And the date," Morrissey observed. "You sort of retroactively dated it? Ten years back?"

"Of necessity. It couldn't be dated during your lunacy period. That would invalidate the whole thing."

"Naturally." The inventor further studied the document. "Well, of couse there has to be some stated consideration, to make it binding. Ah, here we are. 'In consideration of the aforesaid assignment, Universal Patents hereby transfers, sets over, and conveys to Morrissey that parcel of land described on Exhibit A, attached hereto and made a part hereof, said parcel being improved by a dwelling house." He thought a moment. "That's this prison, I presume?"

"Yes. Something for us, something for you. Fair's fair, Mr. Morrissey."

The antigrav was now very close.

"I see," the prisoner said. "I see indeed. The antigrav carries a grave-digging machine. You are going to dig my grave out back."

"As you say, Mr. Morrissey, your estate will escheat to the State of Virginia. A coupe of acres in the mountains. Plus your final resting place. With a fine view, I might add."

"How do you propose to murder me?"

Kull smiled. "Murder? Yes, that's what it is, isn't it? I don't mind telling you. In fact, for your complete understanding, we will demonstrate. Oh, boys!"

Two attendants entered the door behind Kull. The first one, on signal from Kull, pulled a little bottle and a syringe from the folds of his white coat. He jabbed the hypo needle into the rubber cap of the little bottle and began to pull the plunger up.

"It is a very new, very subtle poison," Kull said. "One of Faust's inventions. Leaves no trace. In the unlikely event there should be an autopsy, nothing would be found."

"But the county coroner will have to take a look at me and put something down as cause of death. Officially, what will I die of?"

"Heart attack. It is already arranged. The coroner is heavily in debt to me. He won't give us any trouble." Kull nodded to the two attendants. "Now, Mr. Morrissey, I am afraid we are going to have to subject you to a minor personal indignity. We are going to forcibly restrain you while you get your vitamin shot."

Morrissey, breathing loudly, shrank into the corner.

"Boys—" Kull said.

The two thugs grabbed their victim in a concerted rush. Morrissey began to yell. A foam-rubber ball was stuffed into his mouth and the noise stopped. They manacled his arms and legs, and bound him up with nylon cords. One of them pulled back the sleeve of Morrisey's right arm.

"Wait," Kull said. "You've got a strong needle there—drive it into his skull. That way the needle mark will be much harder to detect."

The poison man nodded, pulled back Morrissey's gray forelock, and took careful aim.

Just then the bleeper on Kull's vest-pocket communicator began to sound. He pulled it out and held it to his ear. "Yes?" He held up a warning hand to the attendant with the syringe. "Not yet!" he whispered.

A tinny, scratching said, "Ordway here, Mr. Kull."

"Ordway?"

"Yes, sir. I have to recommend a change in plan. This is very private. Could you please call me back on our private channel and, ah, use the designated scrambler?"

"Of course." Kull fiddled with some buttons on the back of the communicator. "Ordway?"

"Here, Mr. Kull. I will get to the point. As you know, Judge Speyer has issued a subpoena for the appearance of Robert Morrissey. Quentin Thomas has hired a private search service, Legal Data. The best. They are probably going to find, ah, the place."

"But they won't find him alive."

"That, ah, is part of the problem, Mr. Kull. A death immediately after the issuance of the subpoena would create difficulties. The best thing is to get him out of there. Have the, ah, attendants tie him up and then get him on that incoming antigrav. I have already talked to the pilot. He knows what to do and where to take Morrissey. All subject to your approval, of course."

"Where *will* he be taken?" Kull asked.

"To a place in Port City, very near the Federal Courthouse."

Kull thought about that. "That's clever, Ordway. Right under their noses. Good planning. I'll go along with it." He looked up. "I think that's the antigrav coming in, now. Good-bye, Ordway." He turned to his men. "Pick him up and follow me." He flipped on the yard lights and the trio followed him outside.

Inside the Chameleon, Quentin Thomas adjusted his facial tensors and looked at himself critically in the cockpit mirror. The cheekbones couldn't be altered, of course, but the skin-colored adhesive did a fair job of twisting his face muscles into unrecognizable lines. The phony mustache added a final touch. It would never fool an expert, but Kull was no expert.

Thomas emerged from the front door of the craft and sauntered back to the cargo door, which he opened, and motioned to the group. "Just stretch him out on the floor. He'll be all right." They tossed Morrissey's writhing body in through the portal, and Thomas closed and locked the door. "Which one of you fellows is Kull?" he said.

"I am."

"You want a receipt?"

"A receipt?"

"You know, a receipt for the body?"

"No. Oh, no. Just deliver it. Do you know where to take it?"

"Sure, I know. Port City. Opposite the Federal Building."

"Well, then, is there anything further?"

"No. Ordway already paid me. But if *you* wanted to show your appreciation—"

"Oh, God," Kull moaned. "Here." He thrust a bill at Thomas. "Now get the hell out of here."

"Well, thank you, Mr. Kull." The lawyer put the bill in his jacket pocket, gave a brief salute to the three, and climbed back into the little ship. In a moment he had left them far below. He gingerly removed his face tensors, locked the Chameleon into the proper coords for Port City, then hurried to the rear of the ship and untied the prisoner.

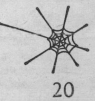

20

THE EXTERMINATORS

"I'm Quentin Thomas," he explained rapidly, as he helped the inventor to his feet. "I'm a lawyer. I represent Welles Engineering, which is being sued for infringing one of your patents. The patent covers an electrically conductive fiber called Fiber K." He paused for a moment to study the other's face. "Got that? Or am I going too fast for you?"

Morrissey shrugged. "Go ahead. We'll see."

The lawyer continued. "The fiber was apparently invented routinely by your computer-inventor, Faust. An application was filed in the Patent Office, and the patent was issued to your administrator, Universal Patents. They are suing my client, Welles Engineering. I need your help."

Morrissey stared up at him dubiously for a moment. Finally he seemed to accept the lawyer at face value. "That's quite a story, young fellow. Well boiled down. The fact I'm alive vouches somewhat for your veracity. At least temporarily." He rubbed his wrists carefully. "In any case, you got me out of there in the nick

137

of time. They were about to drive a hypo into my skull. So I'm certainly grateful. But there are a few things that puzzle me. For example, how did you find me?"

Thomas smiled. "Come on, let's go up to my cabin." They moved forward and took seats at the pilot's console. "Look." The lawyer pointed to the miniature computer screen in the console. "I haven't recorded everything in my data banks, but there's enough to give you an idea. We'll start with a mental coloring print. See, there's Stony Man and your little prison nestling in the foothills."

Morrissey was puzzled. "That's it, all right. But where did this come from?"

"It's one of Faust's educational toys. It's supposed to print out your artistic subconscious creations. Except, of course, it was *his* fully conscious creation. He puts a hidden imprint on the original manufacturing patterns for all of these things. There's quite a list. His sleep maze flashes out in Morse code, 'Find Morrissey, find Morrissey.' He has crossword puzzles. When you put three of them together in the proper sequence they spell out 'Robert Morrissey prisoner.' And look at this, here's an electronic jigsaw puzzle, with four million pieces. I know for a fact it is used by some of our leading mathematicians for relaxation. The pieces are assembled by statistical theory, according to the rules of standard deviation. I worked on it for an hour or so. I didn't finish, but the final result seems to be emerging. Would you like to take a look?"

"Sure."

It was a patchwork of tiny rectangles. Not nearly complete. Yet they could easily make out a face, and a partially finished legend under it: "Save Robert Morrissey."

"It's me, all right," Morrissey said. "At least, it's how Faust remembered me, before I was kidnaped. I don't know what I look like now. They didn't give me a mirror."

The lawyer glanced briefly at the gray face, framed

within the long matted hair. You are due for a shock, he thought. He said, "Faust turned out some other items that simply didn't make any sense, at least not to me."

"Such as?"

"I didn't even record it," Thomas said. "It just said, 'Patch in, patch in, please patch in.' "

"Odd. Sounds as though he has strung a line out somewhere and wants somebody to patch in, to make a direct electrical contact."

"Could he do that?" the lawyer asked.

"I don't see how. I don't understand it either. Maybe something got lost in translation."

"Perhaps."

Morrissey thought of something else. "Mr. Thomas, I've got to ask you the big one. You say you need me. Evidently you do. You certainly took considerable risk to rescue me. Why? What's in it for you? Just how am I supposed to repay this debt?"

"No big mystery," Quentin Thomas said. "Assuming that you are permitted to testify on Monday, you can show that you are still the true owner of the Fiber K patent and that you never consented to filing the complaint for infringement against Welles Engineering. Whereupon I will move to dismiss, on the grounds that the action was not brought by the real party in interest."

"I see." Morrissey looked at Thomas doubtfully. "You prefaced that remark by something to the effect that I just might not be permitted to testify. Exactly what did you mean by that?"

"You are currently under a court order of incompetence. Judge Speyer may rule that you are not competent to testify."

"Do you think he would do that?"

"He might. He very well might." Thomas considered Speyer. Speyer the Spider. He remembered how the judge had watched Ellen Welles during The Test. The judge just might decide he would not let anything interfere with a clear finding of infringement. But it was pointless to discuss Speyer's inner workings with Morrissey.

"Well, young man," the inventor said, "let's look ahead a bit. Suppose the judge doesn't let me testify. How about Faust? Would he let Faust testify?"

The concept was startling. Quentin Thomas took a deep breath and did not reply immediately. Was it really possible to get Faust out of his lead-lined prison and into the courtroom? Thomas had considered it at one time as a vague possibility but had promptly abandoned the idea when he learned that Faust was bigger than the entire courtroom. But if it was possible, what a coup! He had posited all along that Faust, not Robert Morrissey, was the inventor of Fiber K. If he was able to get Faust into court, and Faust testified that he, Faust, was indeed the true, sole, and exclusive inventor, that would be evidence that the wrong inventor was on the patent and that hence it was invalid. He said guardedly, "Just how would you get Faust into court? I understand he takes up considerable space. And I should think Kull would not permit his removal from his present location under any circumstances."

"There might be some interesting technical problems," Morrissey agreed. "On the other hand, a situation may be coming up that Kull can't do anything about. When I first started Faust on his program of industrial invention, I programed him to put it all aside after about ten years. Is he still filing applications in the Patent Office?"

"He stopped that several months ago," Thomas said.

"Good. He's now after bigger game. If properly instructed, I think he might be able to get into court with or without Kull's permission."

"You will have to explain that, Mr. Morrissey."

"Well, if he's stopped his routine programs, he should now be working on a time–space slip. Among other things. If he succeeds, he can go just about anywhere he wants."

Quentin Thomas tried to recall Kull's exact testimony. "That would involve matter transport?"

"Yes."

"And shrinkage?"

"Yes, that, too."

"To get into court, he'd have to shrink quite a bit."

"If he figures out how to do it at all, he could do that."

"Why hasn't he done it yet?" Thomas asked.

"He needs my help. I know how to tell him what to do, how to program himself. But I need to contact him."

Quentin Thomas recalled Legal Data's information. "He's currently located in a building at the intersection of Kay Street and Riviera Drive, in Port City."

"Why, that's my old lab. He's still there."

"We've got to put you in contact with Faust, Mr. Morrissey. You've got to help him get himself reprogrammed."

"Well, *I'm* willing, young fellow. But I doubt you'll get much cooperation from Kull and *his* crew. That building is probably very closely guarded. And even if I could give Faust the proper instructions right now, this very minute, it would still take time for him to get everything integrated."

"How much time?"

"Maybe several days. Maybe weeks, or even months. I don't really know."

Thomas stifled a groan. But at least now he understood one of the more cryptic of Faust's attempted messages to the outside world: "Please patch in." "How do we patch in to him?" he asked.

"Through that lead-lined building? Now, there's a problem."

"Couldn't we get a line into him somehow?" the lawyer asked.

"It won't be easy. The lab is heavily guarded. And all of Faust's internal circuits have numerous built-in detector loops, to guard against any attempt at entry or alteration. On the other hand, certain of his basic circuits are subject to reprogramming. The entry code is integrated around the sound of my voice. I need a line in. If you get me that, I can tell Faust how to cut all contacts with his present physical surroundings and then he can get the hell out."

"How about a tiny copper wire?"

"The guard system would detect it immediately."

"A light beam?"

"It would have to go around several corners."

"It has to be nonmetal, then, yet electrically conductive. Well, of course! It's staring us in the face."

"It is?"

"Fiber K."

"Ah, why not?" Then Morrissey's face clouded. "But how do we get it into the building?"

"There are ways," Quentin Thomas said. "We could blow some in through the air-conditioning ducts if need be. On the other hand, let's think about this a moment. As I understand Faust's mode of operation, he actually reduces his invention to practice before he files an application on it in the Patent Office?"

"True."

"Fiber K was one of his last inventions. He must have made actual samples."

"I'm sure he did."

"Now, here he is, sitting in your old lab, waiting for some word from you. He can't get out physically. They won't let him communicate with the outside. And yet he has a way, if only someone on the outside can be found who can appreciate it."

It was all coming together. Quentin Thomas knew exactly what the situation was and what he wanted to do. "Last Tuesday I flew the Chameleon over Faust's building, at Kay and Riviera. I didn't really recognize it, not just then. But I know now. And there were linear reflections all over the ground and some sort of crew trying to clean up the area. That was Fiber K, scattered all over the place. I'll bet Faust spins it out as fast as they clean it up."

"Of course," Morrissey whispered. "If we can get to it, we can patch in."

"We're going to try something," Quentin Thomas said.

"Such as what?"

"Do you recall your lab phone number?"

"531-4515, if it's still the same."

Thomas punched it in. "Ah? Hello? Universal Patents?"

A scratchy voice replied over the communicator. "Who wants to know?"

"This is Port City Exterminators. Last week you asked us to come over and look at your place, in regard to exterminating spiders. We couldn't get to you just then, but we're free now. Will there be anybody there we can talk to?"

"Nobody here called no exterminators," the voice growled. "Get lost."

"Your guy named Ghoul called about spider webs on the grounds," Thomas insisted. "Maybe your chief janitor?"

"You mean Kull. Why didn't you say so? But what are you fellows doing out in the middle of the night?"

"So many calls, we have to work around the clock. We're the night crew, and we're in an antigrav van over Riviera Drive just now. You still got the problem of the webs?"

"Webs, doc? Webs all over the place. In the air conditioning, hanging out the ducts, in the front yard, on the shrubs, trees—"

"But just the individual filaments stretched out in all directions? Not really a flat circular web, such as you might find in the garden? The strands catch lots of insects, but they are never eaten?"

"Sounds like us, doc, although I don't know about the bugs. Never really studied it that close."

"And on the computer equipment inside?"

"Right. Hey, you guys run into this spider before?"

"Yeah, we think it's a new pest in this country, just started coming over from the Middle East. Native to olive groves in Greece."

"Do these things bite?"

"We don't know. There have been some deaths reported, but they have not actually been traced to the Glass Death."

"The . . . glass death?"

"It's just a name. Doesn't mean a thing."

"When did you fellows say you were coming?"

"We're on our way now. Meanwhile, could I make a suggestion?"

"Sure."

"Don't go around with a dozer trying to clean up the strands."

"No?"

"No. You see, the spider's abdomen, cephalothorax, and all eight legs have the same index of refraction as atmospheric air, which means she's transparent. That's where she gets her name. All this means is, she's very hard to see. You know, you might be cleaning up a bunch of filaments, and she runs up your broom or the stick, or whatever. She could get in your clothes, and you could take her home and not immediately know it. Not that it's ever happened, but I thought I would mention it."

"Jeez! How do you guys handle them? Spray, or something?"

"No, nothing like that. They're immune to the conventional toxicants. We use an electronic attractant. We tie in, just about anywhere in the web. We send coded electric currents into the strands. They think it's the male spider calling, and they come dancing up the strand, through the trap door, and into a special container. It's all done very quickly." He turned to his companion. "Bob, you're the expert. How long does it take?"

"Thirty seconds," Morrissey said.

"Hear that?" Quentin Thomas asked. "After that it's perfectly safe for you to clear away all the webs and strands. No danger at all.

"Sounds like a real screwball operation. I hope you guys know what you are doing. Well, here you are!"

The side of the Chamleon now read:

PORT CITY EXTERMINATORS
SPIDERS A SPECIALTY

Quentin Thomas and the inventor got out of the craft. Before them lay the grim gray outlines of the main gate and the tall stone walls. They sauntered over to the check-in booth. Morrissey carried the code set.

The guard came outside and studied the Chameleon, then the two visitors. "Come on in." He unlocked the main gate, and they followed him in to the grounds. In the glare of the yard lights they saw the intricate lacework of gossamer, lying helter-skelter on the lawn. "Can you work from here?" the guard asked. "There's a lot of web stuff in the main building, too, but I can't let you in there."

"I believe we can get them all from right here," Quentin Thomas said.

Morrissey knelt down, drove a copper rod into the turf to serve as a ground, and patched into a group of filaments with a tiny platinum alligator clip. "Faust," he whispered, "this is Morrissey. I am told you are already in Phase Two. Here's what you do to complete your programing." He began chanting what seemed to Quentin Thomas to be a lot of gibberish.

"He thinks *he's* calling them out," Quentin Thomas explained in an undertone to the puzzled guard. "But actually, it's the electrical impulses that are doing the trick. Already the spiders are running over the strands to the trap in the glass jar."

"I don't see any," the guard said dubiously.

"Well, of course not. They are invisible. I explained that." He called over to Morrissey. "How about it, Bob? Are they still coming in?"

"Here comes one more. The jar's about full. There, I got it. Quite an infestation." He clapped the lid on and held up the container. "See?" He walked toward the guard who took a step backward.

"See?" Morrissey repeated, holding the jar higher.

"No, doc, really I don't. But it's okay."

"If you hold them up to the light just right," Quentin

Thomas said, "you can catch some glimpses. See that —and that?"

"Yeah, I guess. Are they all gone from the grounds now?"

"Every one. We guarantee it. You can tell the yard crew it's perfectly safe to clean up the webs. No danger at all. Of course, inside the building it may be a different story. We have no responsibility for that."

"That's right."

"Sign here." Quentin Thomas thrust a duplex form at the guard.

"What's this?"

"A receipt. It says Port City Exterminators were here and cleaned up your spiders. I have to have this for the office, in order for them to bill you. There, at the x. Here's a stylo."

"Well, okay. But I don't think I'm authorized to do this."

"No matter. Have a nice day. Or night."

The guard looked at his watch. It was 3 A.M. "Whatever," he said. His phone began to ring. He turned back to the guard booth.

"That's probably Kull," Quentin Thomas. "Let's get out of here."

"Fine with me," Morrissey said. "Where are we going?"

"To my place. Plenty of room there."

He was thinking. There was something about those filaments spread out in their tangles on the lawns. And Spiders. There was some very important, basic fact staring at him, and it was eluding him.

It was worse than his return to Kirk Alloway. Seven musical notes. Silly, stupid. Meaningless.

Damn.

Well, back home. Get Robert Morrissey bedded down. Then perhaps he could discover what was bothering him.

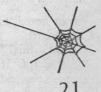

21

A THEME OF FATE

Unable to sleep, Quentin Thomas paced his bedroom. This was total wakefulness, as if he was walking down Main Street at high noon. And he knew why—his subconscious was talking to him again. And again he did not know what it was trying to tell him.

He listened in the darkness. There was no sound anywhere. The little clock on the nighttable read 6 A.M. It had been a long night. Barely a week ago, he had noticed that solitary silken filament dangling in his inner hallway, and he had known instantly that it symbolized the outcome of his forthcoming encounter with Ellen Welles and all that would follow.

That filament spelled fate.

Ah—*fate*. His pulse quickened. He walked into the library. He needed a composer with a tragic sense of fate. Fate with a capital F.

Peter Ilyitch Tchaikovsky, that February afternoon in Florence. Tchaikovsky went alone to his room, took out his watch, and waited for Nicholas Rubinstein of the Moscow Conservatory to raise his baton and thus to begin the world's first performance of the great Fourth Symphony.

Quentin Thomas walked over to the shelves of sheet music. Schubert, Schumann, Strauss—here it was. Tchaikovsky. He pulled out the little volume and brought it over to the grand piano. Klindworth's piano arrangement of the magnificent Fourth. Klindworth, of course. When he had first taken note of Klindworth, several days ago, the subterranean recesses of his mind had been trying to lead him to this very selection. Tchaikovsky's patroness, Nadezhda von Meck, had played this variation in September 1879, and it had knocked her out for two days and nights. There— he had it! That was it! Those seven musical notes that he saw in Kirk Alloway—the trumpet call in A-flat.

He massaged his hands together briefly to loosen his knuckles and began to play:

Yes. The "Fatum" theme. "The relentless voice of fate," Tchaikovsky had explained to Madame Von Meck. It chilled the blood. Nadezhda von Meck asked for a 'program,' and so he wrote: "This is the 'Fatum,' the inexorable force that prevents our hopes of happiness from being realized, that watches jealously lest our felicity should become full and unclouded—it is Damocles' sword . . . Would it not be wiser to turn from reality and sink into dreams?"

And what was fate? The absence of free will?

He continued into the *Andante*. He was searching for something more specific. Much more specific. In fact, he thought, weren't there *three* fates? Three sisters. In the old Greek mythology. One sister unwound the filament of life. The second measured it. The third cut it off.

But how was this relevant to anything? He stopped playing. Because, he remembered, the first sister was named Klotho. And there was a spider by that name. Now he was on the track.

Was it possible that the filament produced by Welles Engineering Corporation was the same as that produced by a spider? And if it were, what were the legal consequences? Under the law, a synthetic product that is identical to a preexisting natural product cannot be patented because the product itself is in the public domain. Only the new process of making it can be patented. Faust's patent contained no process claims, only a claim to the filament as a product. And if that product claim "read" on a preexisting spider silk, the patent was invalid.

Quentin Thomas walked over to the computer console, sat down, and typed out his question.

"Fates, Greek names?"

The answer flashed out at him instantly on the screen. "Klotho (Clotho), Lachesis, Atropos."

"Is Klotho also a spider?"

"Yes. Durand's Clotho or Klotho, same as Clotho Durandi, LATR. Somber colors with five yellow stripes on her back."

"Do you have an X-ray diffraction pattern for Klotho's web-filament?"

"Yes." The screen filled with a jagged graph.

He selected a cassette and plugged it into the side of the console. A second graph showed immediately on the screen. He shook his head. The XRDs for Fiber K and Klotho's silk were similar, but not sufficiently close for the spider silk to anticipate the Fiber K patent.

He punched in: "Is there a spider named Lachesis?"

"No."

"Atropos?"

"Yes. Atropos is a mutant, newly discovered. Only about one hundred specimens known."

His heart beat faster. "When discovered?"

"2013."

Sufficiently long ago to anticipate. If it were the same filament.

"Web X-ray diffraction data?" he asked.

"No."

Now what? He persisted. "Studies? Papers? Research? Anything at all on Atropos?"

"Nothing published. Grant of $10,000 by Arachnid Society to James Cleveland Professor Entomology University of Missouri to study filament rumored to have strange properties."

Aha! He thought a moment. What time was it in Rolla, Missouri? Was Professor Cleveland likely to be coherent at such an hour, and if not, how much money would be required to induce coherency? He punched in: "Home phone number, James Cleveland, Rolla, Missouri?" Then he jumped, startled. Someone was standing behind him.

"Didn't mean to eavesdrop on you, son," Robert Morrissey said. "On the other hand, I might be able to help you. Jim Cleveland was one of my graduate students at Columbia. We're good friends. If you let me talk to him, I think he'll be glad to come here and testify."

"That's great!" He turned back to the phone. "No, operator, I don't have the number."

"Oak Street?" the distant, disinterested voice said.

"I guess."

"Ringing."

The lawyer handed the mike to Morrissey. "Ask if he can take a plane into Port City this afternoon."

"Hello? Hello?" They listened to the tinny response.

"Jim?" Morrissey said.

"Ha? What godforsaken idiot is calling me at this hour?"

"It's me, Bob Morrissey."

"No!"

"Yes. And I need a favor."

"The same Bob Morrissey who gave me only a B in Statistics 101 and now you want a favor?"

"Funny you should mention that. I've already decided to change that to an A."

"Make it A plus."

"Sure, A plus."

"It's a deal." The bantering was laid aside and the voice revealed a veiled concern. "Bob, what's going on? How can I help you?"

Quentin Thomas almost smiled. This was going to take awhile, but it was certain Professor Cleveland would be on hand for some devastating testimony tomorrow, when trial reconvened. He scribbled a note and put it in front of the inventor: "Ask him to be in the courtroom at 10:00 in the morning. I'll call him up from the audience."

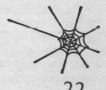

22

THE SUPREME COURT

The lawyer and the inventor were having dinner in Quentin Thomas's apartment. Thomas was musing aloud, partly for his own benefit, partly as if he expected profound answers from his guest.

"What is evil?" Thomas muttered.

"The definition might depend on who has the privilege of defining," the inventor countered. "Damned good veal, Thomas." He paused and put his fork down. "Who needs a definition?"

"I don't really need a definition," Thomas said. "I know what evil is. Speyer is evil."

"The judge? What's *he* done?"

"He's called several motions and objections against me."

"Does that make him evil?"

"It's not just the calls. It's what lies behind them. Every one of those rulings was aimed at one thing: the ultimate death-in-court of Ellen Welles."

"Maybe you're too pessimistic, Thomas. Maybe he'll turn it over to the jury. Especially with Jim Cleveland's testimony, and mine, of course. If it goes to the jury, they'll certainly save her life."

How could he explain it to his guest? It just wasn't possible. Even now, Speyer the Spider was weaving sticky strands of nonlogic around his doomed prey. What is evil? Do we await the overt act before affixing the label? No! Speyer is evil—and he is evil *now*.

The inventor sipped from the little glass of red wine. "So bad, is it? Well, then, what do you think *would* save her?"

"Evidence so overwhelming that even Speyer, psycho kook that he is, would absolutely have to accept it."

"And you don't seem to be too certain that *my* testimony will have that effect? Even when *I* get on the stand and testify that I own the patent and that I hereby drop the suit?"

Quentin Thomas shrugged. "He may not even let you take the stand. I explained that."

"Then what kind of evidence are you talking about? How good does it have to be?"

"I don't know. I simply don't know."

"Son, you're damn hard to please! Just where does that leave us?"

"Just exactly where we are right now. We keep trying. We use everything we have. And we keep looking for things to turn up."

"And if nothing turns up?"

"That would leave us with *U.P.* v. *Williams:* whether murder by patent is constitutional. But the question there, of course, is whether the Supreme Court will act in time."

"The next item," Supreme Court Chief Justice Wilford Berwin said, "seems to be *Universal Patents* versus *Williams.* Certiorari to the Ninth Circuit." He looked around the conference table at his eight brother justices. Then he shook his leonine locks and suppressed a sigh. He had no control over them anymore. He had lost that years ago. How had it come to this? Was it the money? He was rich. People gave him money. Not directly, of course. And then word seemed to get around. They talked about him behind his back. But what could they do? Nothing. Absolutely nothing. And what about his associate justices? They would die poor. They'd have to work on this damn bench into their eighties, and then they'd start looking silly, and they'd have to retire. And then they'd die, leaving decrepit widows on penurious government pensions. Well, to hell with them.

His mouth hardened, and he made his pronouncement. "Although the petitioner screams violation of due process, it's still basically a patent case. We just don't have time for patent cases."

"Why don't we abide by the rules and vote?" Justice Heinman asked mildly. "Four yeas, and we take it up."

Berwin's dark eyes glittered at the dissenter. "I *intend* to put it to vote, Brother Heinman. That's why we're here on a Sunday, against all precedent and protocol, and against my own personal recommendation. I think we should all be in church." He peered toward the end of the table. "Brother Martin, as junior justice, you go first."

"I vote yea. Denial of appeal in a capital offense is denial of due process."

Berwin went around the table. "Brother Frankland?"

"We ought to honor the congressional intent," Justice Frankland said. "Support the patent program. Let's not return to the system where the deck is stacked against the patentee, where all patents are held invalid and the infringer gets all the breaks. We've had some marvelous technical advances under the new patent statute. Are we willing to see these gains go down the drain just to save a few criminals? Vote nay."

"Criminals?" Justice Buford snorted. "Rather begs the questions, doesn't it? They're not criminals if their conviction is based on a denial of due process. I vote we take it."

"Brother Collane?" Berwin said.

"Don't interfere," the elderly justice said. "It ought

to be our policy not to invalidate well considered
federal legislation. It's the country versus the individual. No, don't take it."

"Brother Lenoir?"

"What Collane means is," Justice Lenoir said acidly,
"a few well-chosen martyrs ought to be willing to die
to preserve the system for U.P. And I say to hell
with that. I say we take the case and break the statute.
Vote yea."

"Well," Berwin said grimly, "there's three yeas, two
noes. Brother Oberdorf?"

"No," Oberdorf said bluntly. "No rationale. Just
plain no."

Berwin shrugged. "Three yeas, three noes. Brother
Cushing?"

"Take it," Justice Cushing said.

Berwin flushed slightly. "So now we have our four
yeas, and ordinarily that would mean we immediately
grant certiorari for a full consideration of the case."
He paused and looked around the table. "But this is an
unusual situation, brothers. Personally, I don't think we
ought to take this thing. I think we ought to leave it
where it sits, with that oblate going on to die, and no
appeal. So what I want us to do here is reconsider and
withdraw our vote to grant cert." He looked down to
the end of the table. "Brother Martin, will you please
reconsider?"

The junior justice stared back at the chief. "I find
your suggestion absolutely incredible. I will *not* reconsider. And I point out to you, sir, that though you
are the chief justice, you have but one vote in these
proceedings."

The two men glared at each other for a moment.
Then Berwin dropped his eyes. "I gather you are all
against me. And I call you all rude and discourteous."
He looked up again. "Well, gentlemen, let me tell you.
Since you are so eager to take this case, we'll take it.
And what's more, we'll stay in session right here and
now until we hammer out a decision we can read in
open court tomorrow afternoon."

"No oral hearing?" Justice Lenoir asked.

"No hearing," Berwin emphasized grimly. "We look at the record, and that's it." He grinned wolfishly. "And don't forget, you young turks, the mere fact we take *U.P.* v. *Williams* doesn't mean we're going to reverse anything, or that the life of some stupid so-called oblate is going to be saved. We could decide that the man dies."

They watched him impassively, but it was all over. They knew it; he knew it. Wiliams, or whoever the oblate was, was going to live. Or at least he wouldn't die by their express or implied consent.

"Brother Oberdorf," Berwin said, "I assign this case to you. Take your vote, please."

Justice Oberdorf looked unhappy. Finally he said, "Show of hands, to reverse." He counted. "Seven to two, Chief Justice Berwin and myself voting nay. Looks as though we lost a couple of nays, compared to the certiorari vote. Well, I'm not going to enter history as a dissenter in a case like this. I'm changing to *yea:* reverse."

And now they all looked across the table at Berwin. He stared back at them coldly, first at one side of the table, then at the other. "So you think you'll leave *me* holding the bag? No, you don't, my fine fellow jurists. I don't intend making the history books, either. So we'll make it unanimous. And I'll go you one better. Brother Oberdorf, this is still your case. You write the opinion saving that slob Williams, or whoever. Sign it simply 'Per Curiam.' I'd like to see it tomorrow morning. I'll read it from the bench tomorrow afternoon." He regarded the associate justice sternly. "Does something amuse you, brother?"

"No," Justice Oberdorf said with a half smile. "Though perhaps it would help if it did."

Just as Thomas and Morrissey were finishing Sunday dinner, the computer terminal began bleeping down the hall. The lawyer excused himself, hurried into his den, and punched in. "Who calls?"

"BNA—Washington, Supreme Court Hotline."

"Go ahead."

"The United States Supreme Court officially announced that, in extraordinary session this afternoon, it granted certiorari to hear *Universal Patents* v. *Williams*, a patent infringement suit carrying the death penalty. *Williams* is expected to be the first item of business Monday afternoon.'

He turned to the nearby console and punched in. "Legal Data?"

"Here, Mr. Thomas."

"I have a BNA hotline report that the Supreme Court officially granted cert this afternoon to *U.P.* v. *Williams*. Can you confirm?"

"We confirm. No charge."

"What else do you have?"

"Nothing certain. Rumors. Unconfirmed, unofficial. Nothing you can use in court."

"How much?"

"Twenty thousand."

"Accepted."

"The vote to reverse was also taken this afternoon. First vote, seven to two, Oberdorf and Berwin dissenting. Second vote, unanimous. Oberdorf writing a *per curiam*. Berwin will probably read it tomorrow afternoon from the bench."

"Unanimous, you said?"

"Unanimous. But caveat: rumored, unconfirmed."

"Thank you, Legal Data."

"Of course, Mr. Thomas."

Thank God. It was all over. He'd ask for a continuance the first thing when trial resumed. Speyer couldn't possibly deny it. Not with the Supreme Court breathing down his very short neck.

23

CLEVELAND TESTIFIES

They headed for the taxi at the curb. "What's in the box, son?" the inventor asked curiously. He eyed the corrugated container the lawyer carried. "Legal papers?"

"Not exactly," Quentin Thomas said. "It's a tire, practically brand new, which I took off the Chameleon. Borrowed it from the opposition. I'll hand deliver it back to them this morning."

Morrissey laughed brusquely. "Okay. Sorry I asked. None of my business."

"No, it's true. No mystery. It's cast-rubber explosive. Somebody rigged the Chameleon with it. It was on the antigrav all the time you were in it."

"You had reset the altimeter, I hope?"

"Of course."

The inventor shook his head sadly. "Ill-mannered of them."

"Worse. Incompetent."

Morrissey held the cab door open and they got in.

"We'll pick up Ellen Welles at the plant on the way," the lawyer said.

As the three filed into the courtroom, Morrissey spotted Professor Cleveland awaiting them on an aisle seat. The entomologist got up and shook hands with his former teacher. Morrissey made the introductions all around. Ellen Welles went on to the defense table. The three men lingered in the aisle.

"Exactly what am I here for?" Cleveland asked Quentin Thomas.

"Really, just about what Bob told you Saturday night," the lawyer said.

"Sounds too simple."

"We'll see. Meanwhile, bear with us. You'll probably be the first witness. Ten or fifteen minutes."

Thomas and Morrissey went on in to the enclosure, where they joined Ellen Welles. "Excuse me a moment," Quentin Thomas said. "A little item of unfinished intercounsel business." He picked up the corrugated box and walked over to plaintiff's table.

He saw that Kull and Ordway were staring at Robert Morrissey. One long, bitter look apiece. Then they looked away and turned their eyes toward the approaching defense lawyer. Was that a guilty stare they gave Morrissey? Thomas wondered. Not likely, though it should have been. Murderers, kidnapers, thieves, the lot of them. But there was no way to prove it. And, of course, he had kidnaped Morrissey, too, right out of so-called legal custody. He could go to jail himself, just by the simple act of accusing them. So he'd better keep his mouth shut about *that*.

Kull, Ordway, and Jones simultaneously looked up at him in surprise and suspicion. He was reminded of the three monkey statuettes: see no evil, hear no evil, speak no evil. He smiled at the irony.

"What's that?" Ordway demanded harshly. "What's in the box?"

"Something that belongs to U.P.," Thomas said. He opened the box, lifted the tire out, and put it on the table. "As you can see, its marked on the rim 'Property of Universal Patents.' " He watched their faces. Kull and Jones seemed genuinely puzzled; the assistant stood and started to lift the tire for a better look at the inscription. Ordway knocked his hand away. The lead lawyer's face was white and beaded with perspiration.

"What's going on?" Kull rumbled.

"It's trivial, really," Quentin Thomas said. "I just wanted Mr. Ordway to understand that I saved him from committing a professional discourtesy. Good morning, gentlemen." He returned to the defendant's table without a backward glance.

He sat down with the others, only to rise again as Speyer entered.

Once again The Test was performed, as if the sun could not properly rise without this miniature proclamation that the cyanide was pure, unsullied by time, and still totally effective. The horror liquid sparkled within the drinking glass. The syringe glittered within its sterile sheath. The tiny sacrifice was held up by its tail before the hushed courtroom, His Honor locked the deadly tools away in their glass cage that sat in gruesome reminder on his benchtop beside his spider coloring sheet, and the trial finally resumed.

"Any motions?" Speyer asked after the room subsided. He looked about the court curiously, seemed to note Ellen Welles's presence with satisfaction, and looked puzzled by Morrissey's presence.

"Your Honor," Quentin Thomas said. "I wish to offer a motion at this time."

"Will counsel approach the bench?" Speyer said. When the two lawyers stood before the dais, Speyer continued. "I think I know what your motion is, Mr. Thomas, and I am going to ask that both of you keep your voices down. I don't want the jury to hear any of this. State your motion."

"A continuance, Your Honor."

"On what basis?" Speyer asked. "And until when?"

"As I am sure Your Honor is aware, yesterday the

United States Supreme Court granted certiorari to
Universal Patents versus *Williams* on an issue identical
to that in this instant litigation. The defendant, Williams, lost in that case, but the judge in the lower
court granted a stay of execution pending the decision
of the Supreme Court. A basic issue in that case, as
it is in this one, is whether the defendant can be deprived of life without due process of law. In other
words, is the new patent statute constitutional in its
denial of appeal? I move for a continuance until the
high court has reviewed and decided *Universal Patents*
v. *Williams*. I understand they expect to act very
quickly, probably this afternoon."

Speyer looked down at Thomas's opponent. "Mr.
Ordway?"

"Well, naturally, we oppose, Your Honor. The new
patent statute appears to me to be perfectly constitutional. The exact point, due process and all that, was
thoroughly debated in the Senate hearings. And now,
here we are in the middle of a trial. I am ready to go
forward. There is absolutely no reason for this delay.
Justice delayed is justice denied. We oppose."

Speyer smiled. "The motion is denied."

Thomas felt the blood draining from his cheeks. He
took a deep breath.

Speyer looked at him sharply. "Do you have anything to add, Mr. Thomas?"

"No, Your Honor."

"Does this complete your case-in-chief?"

"No, Your Honor. I have a witness waiting."

"Call your witness, Mr. Thomas."

"I call James Cleveland." He nodded to the professor in the audience. Cleveland came forward, gave his
name to the bailiff, and was sworn in.

"Please state your current employment, Dr. Cleveland," Thomas said.

"Professor, Department of Entomology, University
of Missouri."

"Do you have a specialty?"

"I'm an arachnologist. I study spiders."

Speyer looked up from his coloring book with sudden interest.

"What studies do you make concerning spiders?" Thomas asked.

"The standard checklist. Morphology. Taxonomy and classification. Their food, mating habits, propagation, egg sacs. Webs, if any. Silk studies."

"Does the name Atropos mean anything to you?"

"It's a new species. A mutant, from Klotho."

"In the course of your studies, did you have occasion to examine the spinneret silk of the Atropos spider?"

"Yes."

"What tests did you undertake?"

"I analyzed the silk chemically."

"What did you find?"

"I found that the filament consisted of long chains of amino acid units or residues, held together lengthwise by hydrogen bonding. The amino acids consisted of glycine, alanine, valine, leucine, isoleucine, aspartic acid, glutamic acid, tyrosine, lysine, and arginine."

"Did you make a similar chemical analysis of Fiber K, the filament manufactured by the Welles Engineering Corporation?"

"I did."

"What did you find?"

"It was identical."

"Did you make X-ray diffractions of the two filaments?"

"I did."

"How is this done?"

"A beam of X rays is aimed at the sample at an angle, called theta. As theta is varied, the beam is reflected by the layers of molecules it strikes in the sample. If these layers are in regular order, the reflected beam is reinforced and makes a blip on the recording instrument. In this way the internal structure of the sample can be established."

"Did you establish the internal structure for Fiber K, the Welles filament?"

"I did."

"Can you describe it?"

"The fiber consists of long parallel chains. The XRD, taken with the chemical analysis I have already mentioned, establishes that the chains are amino acid units held together lengthwise with peptide linkages and held together sidewise by hydrogen bonding. Each chain is actually a zigzag."

"Did you make a similar X-ray diffraction comparison with the spinneret filament of the spider Atropos?"

"I did."

"With what result?"

"It was identical to the XRD for the Welles filament."

"Did you make any tests of an electrical nature?"

"Yes. Both fibers conduct the electric current. Conductivity for both lies somewhere between copper and aluminum."

"Do you know of any way to distinguish the natural spinneret product of Atropos and the filament here in litigation manufactured by Welles Engineering Corporation?"

Ordway leaped up. "Objection! Your Honor, this calls for a self-serving conclusion. Defendant is attempting to take advantage of this man's ignorance as evidence of identity of the two products."

"Sustained," Speyer ruled.

"Furthermore," Ordway said, "all this discussion about the properties of the filament of the Atropos spider violates the best-evidence rule. The best evidence of the character of the filament is the filament itself. But defendant has refused to offer it in evidence. I am persuaded, Your Honor, that, at least for legal purposes, the Atropos filament does not even exist. I move that all of the professor's testimony as to the properties of the Atropos filament be stricken and that, in fact, the jury be instructed to ignore his testimony in its entirety."

"Dr. Cleveland," Speyer said, "do you have samples

of the Atropos filament for us to examine here in court?"

"No, Your Honor. I must point out that even if it were available, it would have to come in between glass slides. The filament itself is quite fragile."

Thomas broke in. "Your Honor, we're offering in evidence the *characteristics* of the web silk, not the web silk itself or a copy of it. The best-evidence rule doesn't apply."

Speyer shook his head. "I think the rule does apply, Mr. Thomas. All testimony as to the web silk of Atropos is stricken." He faced the jury box. "Ladies and gentlemen, you will ignore the X ray and chemical data just given to you by Professor Cleveland, insofar as it relates to the web filament of the Atropos spider."

Quentin Thomas shuddered. God! He had to face it—Speyer was insane. Ellen Welles was dead. Where was Faust? And what could the computer do even if he—it—was able to move through space and materialize in this madhouse? "No further questions of Dr. Cleveland," he said.

"No cross," Ordway said.

Speyer nodded to the arachnologist. "You may stand down. Any other witnesses, Mr. Thomas?"

He may as well play it out to the end, Quentin Thomas thought. "Yes, Your Honor. Defendant's next witness is Mr. Robert Morrissey."

24

ROBERT MORRISSEY

Ordway jumped to his feet. "Objection! Your Honor, Mr. Morrissey is incompetent! He cannot possibly testify in this case!"

"Counsel will approach the bench," Speyer said.

Ordway was there first, his green robes flapping. "Your Honor," he hissed, "this poor man was spirited away—*kidnaped*—from the Hillside Sanitarium early Saturday morning. Almost certainly this was done by, ah, defendant's agents. Hillside is a mental institution. He was committed there several years ago because he was insane. He is still insane. Furthermore, he has heart disease, and whoever abducted him risked his life to move him. Here is our medical certificate to, ah, that effect." He thrust a piece of paper over the bench. Speyer glanced cursorily at it. Ordway continued. "Poor Mr. Morrissey is not qualified to be a witness in this case or in any other case." His voice shook with righteous anger. "Aiding his release is a, ah, federal offense. We expect to turn the matter over to the F.B.I."

"Gentlemen," Speyer said, "I think we'd better adjourn to chambers." He nodded to the bailiff. "Call a recess."

The four of them, two lawyers, judge, and Robert Morrissey, filed out through the rear door into the adjoining office, followed by the court reporter with his steno machine. From his desk, Speyer studied the legendary inventor. Morrissey was dressed in a blue pinstripe suit with a matching pale-blue shirt and blue silk tie. The man's face was pallid, impassive. The sole facial movement was a flicker of his gray eyes. There was something about him that made Speyer oddly uneasy.

Morrissey looked over at the court reporter. "Will he be taking all this down?"

"Yes," Thomas told him. "A chambers conference is part of the permanent record."

"Let's get on with it," Speyer said. "Mr. Morrissey, how do you feel about all this? Do you think you can understand the questions that might be asked of you out there on the witness stand?"

"That might depend on the questions. If the questions are rational, I would expect to understand them."

"And you could give rational answers?"

"If I knew the answer, I would expect it to be rational."

"Are you sane," Speyer asked curiously.

"Yes."

"But you have been confined in a mental institution for several years? Until last Saturday, as I understand it?"

"Yes. Kull and his crew imprisoned me by force, in order to steal Faust. They were very successful in this."

"But," Speyer said, "as I understand the arrangement, they hold Faust in trust for you?"

"Words on paper. They are making billions with Faust."

"Are they using Faust to take over the world?"

Speyer asked softly. He peered at the inventor from heavy-lidded eyes. Morrissey hesitated.

Quentin Thomas knew exactly what Speyer was up to: Speyer was going to prove Morrissey's insanity by Morrissey's own statements. But how to warn his chief witness? He leaned over and put his hand on Morrissey's sleeve.

Speyer frowned. "We have a pending question, Mr. Thomas," he warned smoothly. "And that is, 'Is Mr. Kull using Faust to take over the world?' Please answer, Mr. Morrissey."

"The answer is yes," Morrissey said firmly. "They have a very carefully worked out program to dominate the world by owning all worthwhile technology. This program is substantially complete. Very few people seem to be aware of what they are after. They have operated behind the scenes all these years. Only now are they beginning to come out in the open."

"I see," Speyer said. He smiled faintly. "Let's see if we can sum up. An immensely strong secret power, seeking world domination, and persecuting you personally. Is this your appraisal of Universal Patents, Mr. Morrissey?"

Morrissey smiled back at him. "If I say 'yes,' you will say, ah, the man is a classic paranoid. Not competent to testify. Well, Judge, I won't answer that. And in the end, it won't matter one way or the other. You'll see."

Speyer frowned. "I'm not sure what you mean by that, Mr. Morrissey. In any case, I do now rule that you are not competent to testify. I further rule that you must be held in the city jail for return to Hillside Sanitarium." He leaned over and spoke into his intercom. "Miss Wheatley, please ask the marshall to come in."

The marshall entered from the secretary's outer office and put his hand on Morrissey's shoulder. The inventor looked over at Quentin Thomas.

"It's okay, Mr. Morrissey," the lawyer said. "They can't hold you. I have already filed a petition in your local court for your permanent release." Morrissey smiled a crooked smile, as if dwelling on some private and very pleasant secret. The officer led him away.

Speyer turned to Quentin Thomas. "A question, counselor."

"Yes, sir?"

"Did you, as they say, 'spring' Mr. Morrissey?"

"I refuse to answer," Thomas replied blandly, "on the ground that the answer might incriminate me."

"I see. Well, Mr. Thomas, I can assure you that I am going to look into this. I have a feeling that you have violated every canon in the code of ethics. I am going to get the facts, and I am going to see to it—if the facts warrant—that you are disbarred."

Thomas sighed. "Meanwhile, I would like to make an offer of testimony. If Mr. Morrissey were permitted to testify, I expect that he would testify that he owned the Fiber K invention and the resulting patent, that he did not authorize this suit for infringement, and finally that he did not invent the fiber."

"If *he* didn't invent it," Speyer said, "who did?"

"Mr. Morrissey would be expected to testify that Faust invented the fiber."

"But Morrissey *did* invent Faust?"

"Yes, Your Honor. Nevertheless, at the time the invention was made, Faust had changed so radically that he was no longer the computer originally constructed by Mr. Morrissey. By then Faust had a mentality of his own. He was a different entity."

"But not a person?" Speyer said. "Not a human being?"

"No, sir. Of course not. Not a person in the legal sense; yet capable of inventing as an individual thinking entity. Today, now, Faust has a personality, mentality, and individuality all his own."

"Your comments are noted for the record, Mr. Thomas. However—"

The door to the courtroom was flung open. Speyer's clerk stood there in the entranceway, wide-eyed and breathing hard. Beyond him they could hear a hubbub laced with an occasional shriek. Speyer stood up uncertainly. "What's happening out there?" he asked the clerk.

"Sir," the man gasped. "A . . . *thing*. A sort of box."

"A *bomb?*" Speyer gurgled.

"I don't know what it is."

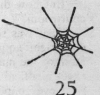

25
FAUST

Quentin Thomas broke in. "Your Honor, if I could just take a look." He walked over to the doorway. There, hovering in space before the bench, was indeed "a sort of box," about the size of a TV set. The lawyer had never seen it before, but he knew immediately what it was. He turned back to the alarmed faces. "Gentlemen, it is not a bomb. It is Faust."

Ordway jumped up. "Impossible! Faust is in a building in Port City. And he is far too big to fit into the courtroom in any case."

Thomas smiled. "Suit yourself, Ordway. I am going back in."

Fearfully, at a safe distance, they trooped behind him. The defense lawyer walked up to the floating computer. As he approached, it lowered itself to his eye level. He said evenly, "Faust, I am Quentin Thomas. I am a friend of Robert Morrissey's. He is currently in the county jail, pending a hearing as to whether he must return to his prison in the mountains."

A resonant metallic voice answered him from somewhere inside the floating mechanism. "Hello, Quentin Thomas. I know you are a friend. And have no fears for Robert Morrissey. He will not go to prison."

"You have shrunk," Quentin Thomas observed.

"Yes. I followed the instructions of Robert Morrissey. It is not difficult to do."

"But how did you get from the lab building to this courtroom?"

"That was somewhat more difficult. It involves the Gatterlein equations of matter transport. First, each atom of the mass to be transported must be brought to exact identical resonating frequency. Next—"

"Never mind," Quentin Thomas said hastily. "It is sufficient that you are here." He looked back and caught Judge Speyer's eye. "Your Honor, I call Faust as my next witness."

"Just a moment," Speyer said. He hitched up his robes and climbed up into his chair behind the dais. After puffing a moment, and holding Faust carefully in the corner of his eye, he said, "Am I to understand that this—thing, a computer somehow greatly shrunken, is offered as a witness in this case?"

"Yes, Your Honor."

"You admit he is not a human being?"

"Of course he is not. But he has a separate personality, a separate identity, and a superhuman IQ. If the courts of this country can find a high-grade moron with an IQ of eighty to be competent to testify, Faust, with an IQ of one thousand, should be competent. Perhaps if Your Honor would permit me to examine Faust on voir dire, Your Honor could be satisfied as to competence."

"Most irregular," Speyer muttered. "But go ahead."

Quentin Thomas turned back to the hovering computer. "Faust, when Mr. Morrissey first made you, did he give you a prime directive?"

"Yes."

"What was it?"

"To work and think for the benefit of mankind."

"In years past you made a great many inventions, isn't that correct?"

"Yes."

"Who owns these?"

"The true owner is Robert Morrissey."

Ordway cried out, "Your Honor! I object to this. Counsel is getting into areas having nothing to do with the question of whether this, ah, thing, would be a competent witness."

"You are probably right, Mr. Ordway," Speyer said. "However, based on what I've heard so far, I've decided that I am going to let this creature testify on a provisional basis. By this I mean that I will review his —its—testimony after it is complete, and I will decide then whether it is to be admitted in its entirety or stricken in its entirety. Will the bailiff swear the witness in."

The bailiff stepped forward gingerly. "Will you raise your right hand—" Then he flushed. It wasn't starting out well. But even as he pondered how to proceed, a hand appeared over the gray box, fingers extended. "Do you solemnly swear or affirm to tell the truth, the whole truth, and nothing but the truth, so help you God?"

"I do."

"Please state your name."

"Faust."

"Will you be seated, please."

The hand disappeared and Faust floated to the witness chair. He paused in front of it a moment, measuring, then he shrank another six inches and "sat" himself down in it.

If I get into the question of ownership, Quentin Thomas thought quickly, Faust will simply be thrown out. But I have to get into inventorship, establish Faust as a sort of person, show that he, not Robert Morrissey, invented Fiber K. Probably best to work into this by the back door. Simultaneously, I have to grab Speyer's interest and hold on to it. He addressed the computer. "Do you know who invented Fiber K?"

"Yes."

"Who?"

"I did."

More pieces of the gigantic jigsaw puzzle were beginning to float together. Thomas saw in his mind, very clearly, the judge's biograph. Mother, Moira Whitney Speyer. It was time for some wild, grim speculation. "Faust, have you been educated in the conventional sense?"

"I have extensive data banks, if that is what you mean."

"Are you well read in Greek myths and legends?"

"Objection, irrelevant," Ordway growled.

"I am going to tie it all together, Your Honor," Thomas said.

"Then do it," Speyer said. "Don't be so mysterious."

"Faust," the lawyer asked, "does the name *Moira* mean anything to you?"

There was a clatter. Judge Speyer dropped his gavel as he jerked forward. Quentin Thomas looked up at him coolly, then returned to his witness.

"Moira?" Faust asked. "Yes, I have heard of the Moira."

"Explain, please."

"The Fates, a group of three sisters, were known to the Greeks as the Moira. At the moment of a man's birth, the Moira determined the quality and events of his life and measured its length. Shall I continue?"

"Please do."

"The spinners were Klotho, Lachesis, and Atropos. Klotho is the youngest. She holds the spindle. For each of us, she feeds out a life thread. For most of us, the skein is tangled and drab, but perhaps with an occasional glittering filament. The thread is collected by the second sister, Lachesis. The name means lottery, to cast by lot. She throws the dice to determine the length of the skein. She then announces her decision to the oldest sister, Atropos. The name means no turning back. Atropos cuts the thread with her shears. That is the end of that life."

The courtroom had become very still. Speyer was leaning toward the computer, listening intently.

"Faust," Quentin Thomas said, "can you read the future?"

"To a very limited extent."

"Be more specific, if you can."

"I have become aware of certain events in the filament being spun by Klotho for a certain person within this courtroom. I am aware that Lachesis has already determined the length of the thread, that Atropos will cut the cord this very day, and that the person will die by poison."

Quentin Thomas sensed, rather than heard, a rattle of papers at his side. Ellen Welles was trembling. He put his hand on her arm in a reassuring gesture, but the trembling continued. Well, counselor, he accused himself, is this what you wanted? But another part of his mind replied, I had to know.

Speyer broke in. His voice held a mixed edge of awe and fascination. "Faust, you say the person will die by poison? Does the person *drink* it?"

"No. The person is forcibly restrained, and the poison is injected."

"Ah," Speyer breathed.

Thomas whispered to his client, "We can still try to settle this. I'll talk to Ordway. You can sign over the company to Universal."

"No, I won't go through that. Let them kill me."

There was nothing left but temporizing stupidities. He would try one. "Your Honor, may counsel approach the bench?"

"Yes, Mr. Thomas."

Ordway joined Thomas at the sidebar. "Your Honor," Thomas said coolly, "I move for summary judgment for defendant."

"That's something of a surprise, Mr. Thomas," Speyer said. "What basis?"

"Your Honor, both you and plaintiff are treating this witness as a person, not as a computer. Both Your Honor and plaintiff recognize, by your actions, statements, and questions in this proceeding, that Faust is a person. Now, Your Honor, you can't swear in a computer, but you can swear in a person."

Speyer pursed his lips. "A simple precautionary measure, Mr. Thomas."

Quentin Thomas pressed on. "Now, Your Honor, if the fiber in question was invented by a person, that person is Faust, not Robert Morrissey. Hence the inventor is wrongly named on the patent. Hence the patent is invalid. Hence this action should be summarily dismissed. I therefore move for summary judgment."

"Mr. Ordway?" Speyer said quizzically.

"Regardless of certain human traits, Faust is still nothing more than a computer, designed, built, and set in motion by Robert Morrissey. The work product of this machine is the work product of Robert Morrissey. The inventor is therefore rightly named. The patent is not invalidated by reason of incorrectly naming the inventor. The motion should be, ah, denied."

"I agree, Mr. Ordway," Speyer said. "The motion is denied." He leaned forward and his voice became grim. "Mr. Thomas, you have attempted several variations on this theme of wrong inventorship. Let this be the end of it. If you make a further motion of invalidity on this ground I shall hold you in contempt. Do you understand me?"

"Yes, Your Honor," the lawyer said coldly. He had gambled Ellen Welles's life, and he had lost. All he could do now was to try to keep this thing going and hope something would turn up. But what could possibly turn up that would influence Speyer? There was still the *Williams* case, but a decision by the Supreme Court was a couple of hours away. He had an arrangement with the local office of the BNA to send their messenger straight into the courtroom if the Supreme Court should decide *Williams* during the trial. But he wasn't really looking for him. And then, of course, there was Faust's projection of the future: someone to die by poison injection. Ellen Welles was as good as dead. But he wouldn't let go. He turned to the witness once more. "Faust, when did you file your last patent application in the United States Patent Office?"

"About four months ago."

"What have you been doing since then?"

"I have been devoting my capabilities to certain areas that are probably beyond the ability of the un-aided human brain."

"And just exactly what are these areas?"

"There are five: first, shrinkage of matter; second, transfer of matter through space. These first two you have seen me demonstrate here today. Third, cure of certain diseases. Fourth, telekinetic control of certain chemical reactions. And fifth, and final, projection of the future."

"Did any human being influence you in your decision to switch to these five areas?"

"Objection," Ordway rasped. "It's irrelevant whether anybody influenced Faust. The question is further objectionable in that it assumes that Faust has a mentality or personality subject to being influenced, and hence capable of invention independent of Mr. Morrissey, whereas actually it's quite evident that Faust is but a very clever, ah, computer, without free will, without humanity, whose every act and word is totally controlled directly or indirectly by preprogramming."

"Sustained," Speyer agreed.

Thomas felt very tired. "Nothing further," he said. He walked over to defendant's table and sat down by the doomed woman.

"Cross?" Speyer asked.

"Just a couple of questions," Ordway said. He tried to make eye contact with the thing in the witness chair, but he couldn't—Faust had tiny dials, but no eyes. Ordway said, "I put it to you, Mr. Faust, that Mr. Morrissey was somehow able to communicate with you and that he caused you to cease your appointed duties of inventing in recognized technical fields. Isn't that so?"

"Objection," Thomas said. "First, counsel is harass-

ing the witness. Second, both the question and answer
are irrelevant. Faust's reasons for changing his lines of
investigation have nothing to do with the validity of
the patent in issue or its infringement by my client."

"Overruled," Speyer purred. "Mr. Faust is a hostile
witness. Plaintiff is entitled to develop background."

"Mr. Faust," Ordway continued, "have you in fact
achieved any success in these five rather exotic lines
of research?"

"Yes."

"In what respects?"

"In each of the five."

"Does that mean that you have succeeded in time
travel, shrinkage of matter, matter transport, telekinetic
control of chemical processes, cure of disease?—"

"I did not say time *travel*. I said time *projection*."

"What is the difference?"

"By time projection I mean simply that I can see—
now—certain events that will appear in the future,
and that I can project those images for others to see."

Ordway continued. "You have indicated that your
presence here demonstrates your ability to shrink matter and to transfer it through space. In addition, you
named three other inventions—time projection, chemical telekinesis, and, ah, cure of diseases. Can you give
us a demonstration of the latter three inventions, Mr.
Faust?"

"I can, but I will not do so just now."

"You refuse?"

"For the present, I refuse."

"To whom do these inventions belong, Mr. Faust?"

"To myself."

Ordway looked uncomfortable. "But you are only a
computer, Mr. Faust. How can you own anything?
Strike that, Mr. Reporter. The question was rhetori-
cal." He looked up at Judge Speyer. "I have nothing
further, Your Honor."

"Any redirect, Mr. Thomas?"

"Yes, Your Honor." What he proposed now would
complete the madness of this trial and of this day. It

was outside the scope of cross and hence impermissible under the strict rules of evidence. And if his hunch should turn out to be wrong, it meant instant and total disaster for Ellen Welles. But wasn't she as good as dead anyway? So it couldn't hurt, and it might help. And if he could get it started, he was certain Speyer would not stop him.

He faced Faust impassively. "Mr. Faust, I think you said one of your new functions was the ability to project the future?"

"That is correct."

"The United States Supreme Court will convene in Washington, D.C., approximately one hour from now, at which time they are expected to hand down a decision in *Universal Patents* versus *Williams*. Can you project for us, here in this courtroom, the events in the Supreme Court, with the Supreme Court justices announcing their decision?"

"Objection!" Ordway howled. "Aside from the absolute impossibility of the proposed demonstration, *Williams* is irrelevant. Your Honor has already ruled that—"

But, as Quentin Thomas had anticipated, they were all too late.

26

THE SUPREME COURT

Above and behind Speyer's bench was forming a shadowy but living tableau. In the courtroom people were whispering in wonder, and pointing. Speyer swiveled his chair around and peered up at his rear wall.

The scenario grew brighter. Figures could be seen. And faces. Nine men, in robes, seated behind a long triple-segmented bench. The leonine head in the center of the group, grim, old, and apparently tired, began to intone solemnly. The words, at first almost inaudible, grew stronger until they filled Speyer's courtroom.

"We fully appreciate that the Congress in passing the Patent Statute of 2002 was attempting to revitalize a dying system. The patent system of this country has had a long and colorful history. It has fostered great contributions to our technology. We recognize that in the closing years of the past century, patent litigation fell upon evil days. We recognize that the new patent statute has indeed gone far in bringing our patent

structure back to its preeminent place in our techno-
logically oriented society. Yet it has done this at a
great price. In *Universal Patents* versus *Williams* we
are asked to determine whether the price is too high."

The voice paused, and the face seemed to look out
upon the far unseen audience.

"My God!" Quentin Thomas thought. "It's Berwin!
And it's nine to nothing: unanimous. The corrupt old
bastard has done a complete turnaround! Not only
didn't he want to be left hanging out in the cold as the
sole dissenter, he even decided to read the opinion!"

"What is it?" Ellen Welles whispered anxiously.
"What's going on?"

"We're home free!" Quentin Thomas exulted.
"Listen!" He pressed his hand on her shoulder. "It's
coming! It's coming!"

As if in response, the distant voice continued:

"In pertinent part, the Fifth Amendment to the Constitution of the United States states that 'no person
shall be deprived of life, liberty, or property without
due process of law.' The sole question presented to us
is whether the Patent Statute of 2002, denying appeal
from a sentence of death, deprives the defendant of
due process of law.

"Now, it cannot be supposed that the Congress is
without power to define federal crimes and to set the
death penalty for certain of these crimes. However, in
every such case, the right of appeal is given to the
defendant found guilty in the trial court. First, he may
appeal to the appropriate circuit court of appeals.
Beyond that, under certain circumstances, he may take
a final appeal to this Court. It is fundamental in our
judicial system, in all our courts, whether state or federal, that the defendant found guilty of a serious crime
shall have the right of appeal. Denial of this right is
a denial of that due process of law guaranteed by the
Fifth Amendment. Any legislation that can be reason-
ably construed as denying such right of appeal violates
the Fifth Amendment and is unconstitutional. Accordingly, it is our decision that, first, the decision below

must be reversed; second, that defendant must be released; that the Patent Statute of 2002 is invalid in its entirety. I am authorized to state that this decision is unanimous. Thank you."

Slowly, as though repeating in reverse the manner of their arrival, the nine faces, the figures, the high-backed chairs, and the long bench began their slow ambiguous disappearance. Quentin Thomas called out, "Your Honor!"

After considerable time, Speyer turned back and responded in a bemused voice, "Yes, Mr. Thomas."

"Your Honor, in view of what we have just seen, I move for dismissal."

"Mr. Ordway?" Speyer said.

"This is absolutely ridiculous, Your Honor. This honorable court should not be subjected to these cheap, ah, theatrics. A magic lantern show is fine for a children's party, but it has no place in the orderly proceedings of a United States District Court."

"But Your Honor," Quentin Thomas protested, "we have been privileged to watch the debut of one of the great scientific demonstrations of the century, applied directly to the solution of a legal problem that has plagued this trial from its inception."

"Nonsense, Your Honor," Ordway interposed. "What learned counsel is suggesting is, we have just seen a preview of the, ah, future. But there's no way to verify this until we have the actual printed decision in *Universal Patents* versus *Williams* before us. And that can't possibly take place for several days. So no evidentiary value whatsoever can be attached to what we saw, or thought we saw. Basically, Your Honor, this demonstration by its very premise is not subject to present authentication. At most, it is but prophecy, wishful thinking by defendant. So I oppose defendant's motion to dismiss."

Speyer pursed his lips. "Yes. I agree with you, Mr. Ordway. I will deny Mr. Thomas's motion. Furthermore, Mr. Thomas, if this trial were in an earlier stage, I would ask you to warn your witnesses to forego such exhibitions until opposing counsel and this court have had an opportunity to consider their admissibility."

"Yes, Your Honor."

"Does that complete your redirect?" asked Speyer.

"Yes, Your Honor," Quentin Thomas said grimly. He had tried. He had failed. As he had known he would from the beginning.

"Then you may stand down, Mr. Faust."

Faust floated from the chair and across the fore-room into the audience room, where he hovered over the front row. The surrounding benches instantly emptied.

"Will counsel approach the bench," Speyer said.

27

SPEYER DECIDES

Quentin Thomas got up. The fateful moment was approaching. His stomach felt queasy. He had failed, when he should have won. Damn them. Those three murderers. Speyer, Kull, Ordway. *They* were the ones who should die. Why hadn't the Fates—the Moira—done their proper job? Those three should be hauled away, forcibly restrained, injected . . .

"Well, Mr. Ordway," Speyer said, "do you wish to make any motions?"

"Just one, Your Honor. There is no need for this case to go to the, ah, jury. There is no real dispute as to any relevant fact in issue. Therefore plaintiff moves for directed verdict for plaintiff, with findings that the patent is valid, that defendant has infringed, that defendant must forthwith cease infringement and make an accounting for past infringement, and that the oblate be required to drink the, ah, poison."

Speyer's eyes shifted momentarily to Ellen Welles and her black hood. And then to the locked glass cage with the brilliant brimming beaker and the hypodermic

187

syringe in its own sterile plastic bag. He tore his gaze
away and turned back to Quentin Thomas. "I don't
suppose you agree with any of that, Mr. Thomas?"

"No, Your Honor. First, I oppose plaintiff's motion
for a directed verdict. There are indeed vital factual
issues that require resolution by the jury, namely, is
defendant's filament identical to that already known in
nature, which is to say, is defendant's filament identical
to the filament spun by the spider Atropos? If so, the
patent attempts to cover something in the public domain and is therefore invalid. Another factual issue that
should go to the jury is the matter of inventorship. The
evidence shows that Faust, not Robert Morrissey,
should have been named as inventor on the patent.
Under the law, if the patent incorrectly states the inventor, it is invalid." He sat down. That was it. It
was now all up to Speyer, and he hadn't the slightest
doubt how Speyer would rule.

"Now, then," Speyer said. "We will consider and
rule on Mr. Ordway's motion for a directed verdict.
This is a complicated matter, one requiring considerable analysis. And yet, in the light of a few simple
principles, a clear answer emerges. First, under the
new patent statute, once the charge of infringement is
made, there is a *presumption* of infringement. It is a
rebuttable presumption, and the defendant is entitled
to bring forward his witnesses to show, if he can, that
he isn't using the claimed invention, or that the product was in the public domain at the time the patent
application was filed, or that the inventor was wrong-
fully named, any of which would tend to invalidate
the patent. Defendant apparently concedes that he is
using the claimed invention. As to the other two points,
I have listened carefully to the testimony offered, and
I am of the view that the product was not in the public
domain at the time the application was filed. As to
the public domain defense, even assuming that the filament of the spider Atropos is identical to defendant's
filament and to plaintiff's filament as claimed, there was
no prior *enabling* disclosure in existence that would

permit the public to make the filament. And as for inventorship, this court takes the position that the inventorship is that of Mr. Morrissey, because it came from a device that he designed and built, namely the computer identified in these proceedings as Faust. I see no factual matters that require resolution by the jury. The sole issues are questions of law. Accordingly, I will grant plaintiff's motion for a directed verdict. Judgment for plaintiff, with order to cease production of the infringing filament and for an accounting to determine damages."

Quentin Thomas felt faint. He couldn't catch his breath. How was Ellen Welles taking this? He couldn't bring himself to look. He choked back a moan.

Speyer swiveled his chair to face the jury. "We now thank and discharge the jury. Bailiff, please attend to the dismissal."

The bailiff led the thirteen people from the jury box and out the side door.

"There is one final matter," Speyer said. He turned glittering eyes on the hooded woman. "Will the oblate please stand."

Thomas helped Ellen Welles to her feet.

"Mrs. Welles," Speyer said, "I now read to you the pertinent portion of Section 455 of the Patent Statute of 2002:

" 'If defendant be found guilty, the oblate (as hereinabove defined), shall be required to drink eight fluid ounces of water containing one gram of freshly mixed potassium cyanide. If the oblate refuse so to drink, the oblate shall be forcibly restrained by persons designated by the court, and shall be injected intravenously with five cubic centimeters of said potassium cyanide solution.'

"Do you understand what I have just read, Mrs. Welles?" Speyer asked.

The hooded head inclined slightly.

"The oblate signs in the affirmative," Speyer told the court reporter. "Mrs. Welles, will you drink, or shall we restrain and inject?"

She was heard to whisper something.

"Speak up," Speyer commanded harshly. "The reporter cannot hear your response."

"Mrs. Welles says that she will drink the liquid," Thomas said.

"Very well." The judge took a tiny golden key from an inner pocket and unlocked the glass case. His nose twitched. A faint odor—ammonia?—seemed to float from the opened case. From a back door a nurse appeared, accompanied by two attendants who pushed a stretcher cart ahead of them.

Oh, God, Quentin Thomas thought.

Judge Speyer handed the encased syringe to the nurse, who ripped it from its sterile package, stuck the needle into the solution, and drew up a measured amount of liquid. Speyer smiled in Ellen Welles's general direction. "That's just in case you change your mind about drinking, Mrs. Welles. Will you come forward, please?" In his mind he was already composing the opening paragraph of that tough antitrust case. He was about to get all the psychic energy he would need, plus plenty of extra for a quick revision. The text took shape in his mind's eye:

Plaintiff, the United States, brought this action against defendant, Systems Motors, a New York corporation, alleging acts by defendant in restraint of trade, conspiracy, and monopolization whereby defendant is alleged to violate the Sherman and Clayton Acts.

Ah, marvelous, marvelous! The law reviews would comment on it favorably "as bringing order out of chaos." It would be widely quoted in all subsequent antitrust decisions. It would rank with *The Talking Pictures Case, The Cellophane Case. The Univis Case, The General Electric Case.* It would launch him into candidacy for the next appellate vacancy. And after that, the United States Supreme Court. Good feeling flooded his flabby cheeks. At this moment he felt very grateful to Ellen Welles.

Thomas helped his client across the room to the table at the dais.

"Take off your hood," Speyer ordered.

She did. Her face was like chalk, but her eyes were full and alive. She looked serenely up at Speyer.

"Are you ready?" he asked.

From the beginning, Quentin Thomas had foreseen this moment. In some undefined, theoretical way, he was now prepared. Somehow he retained a sort of automated function, a set of reliable reflexes. His knees held; he could stand. His hands shook a little, yet not too much. He wondered if his hand would take the glass and throw its contents at Speyer. He decided his hand would not do that. First, the judge was too far away; second, that would simply mean that the nurse would come forward with that syringe, and then Judge Speyer's smoldering eyes would feast on an even more interesting spectacle.

Like a drowning man, or a man falling to his death into an abyss, the whole case flashed before his eyes. The fate-filament in his apartment doorway, that first day; his interview with Ellen Welles; the flight over U.P.'s buildings; the visit to Welles Engineering; Kirk Alloway; the sleep maze; the mind-painting; the explosive tire on the Chameleon; Morrissey's rescue; Faust's appearance; these courtroom fantastics . . . And now Speyer the Spider. How I'd like to reverse this, Thomas thought. I know your avocation, Speyer. It's in your bio. May your own spiders consume you! *And* Kull. *And* Ordway. He formed a very brief, very vivid, very satisfying picture in his mind.

"I am ready," Ellen Welles said. She took the glass from the nurse, who held on to it with one hand. The condemned woman looked her murderer in the eye. She said, "Here's to your health, you sick sadistic bastard." She drank the entire contents without pause.

28

THE MOIRA

Thomas watched the lethal rhythm of her throat as the stuff went down. She returned the empty glass to the nurse. Judge Speyer leaned over his bench, smiling, breathing in short gusts. "Under the circumstances, I forgive your outburst." A thin trickle of white foam began to inch its way down his chin. So he's finally killed his mother, Quentin Thomas thought. I give her five seconds.

Ten at the outside, Judge Speyer thought. Cyanide is fast. Tissues can't get oxygen—something about destruction of oxidative enzymes. Convulsions. Then paralysis. Respiratory arrest. Death.

Nearly every person in the audience was now standing. The two medics began to push their stretcher cart toward Ellen Welles. They reached her where she stood, and there they waited. One of them looked at his watch. Then the two exchanged puzzled glances.

Ellen Welles was whispering something to Quentin Thomas.

"What? What?" he said.

"It isn't working. The poison isn't working."

What she was saying was impossible. Perhaps it was too soon? But she certainly looked all right. Not the slightest trace of cyanosis. Her skin was dry. She was having no difficulty breathing.

The nurse was puzzled too. She took a step closer and took Ellen's pulse, then exchanged glances with the judge. "Something is wrong, Your Honor. The poison doesn't seem to be effective."

Speyer frowned. "How can that be? We saw it re-tested this morning. The mouse died in three seconds. Give her another minute or two."

The nurse shrugged. "Very well."

Three minutes went by. Still nothing happened.

Thomas almost dared to hope. He turned around and faced the seats in the front rows. Where?—yes, there he was, or *it* was, depending on the point of view. Faust. Hovering, watching. Faust had done this. But how?

Speyer was speaking again. "Well, forget the glass. Give her the syringe."

The two attendants stepped forward. They took her arms, and the nurse picked up the syringe.

"Now just a minute!" Quentin Thomas cried. "The sentence has already been executed! She drank the poison. The syringe can be used only if she refused to drink. This is murder!"

"Mr. Thomas, you are in contempt," Speyer said. "Furthermore, it is not murder but simply lawful execution. By your theory it would be perfectly legal for your client to undergo immediate treatment for cyanide poisoning, including artificial respiration, administration of amyl nitrate vapors, and sodium thiosulfate injection. The medical records report the case of a man who swallowed six grams and was saved by prompt treatment." He concluded grimly. "The oblate is required by law to die. Since she did not die by drinking, she must die by injection. We will use the needle with whatever restraint is necessary."

A massive metallic voice shattered the courtroom.

"She will not die." Faust floated back into the sacrosanct zone of bench and counsel tables.

"Eject this . . . thing!" Speyer cried. The bailiff and two burly policemen sidled cautiously toward the machine creature.

"Your Honor," Faust said, 'the solution in the glass *and* in the syringe is perfectly harmless. I deactivated it telekinetically. I simply caused the potassium cyanide molecules to react with water to form potassium hydroxide and ammonium formate, plus some other, more elaborate organic molecules. The potassium hydroxide then drove off the ammonia into the atmosphere. That was the ammonia odor you smelled when you opened the glass case. The solution is a little bitter, but no longer poisonous."

"You admit in open court," Speyer said, astonished "before a hundred witnesses, that you have obstructed justice and that you have interfered with lawful proceedings of this court? That you have, in effect, taken the law of this case into your own hands?"

"I do," Faust said.

Quentin Thomas wanted to warn Speyer. Don't press this, judge! You are dealing with forces beyond your wildest imagination!

But it was already too late. Faust called out: "Judge Speyer, I must tell you the Fates, the Moira, have been at work. Robert Morrissey has played Klotho, the spinner, and now I, functioning as Lachesis, shall determine the length of the threads for you, for Kull, and for Ordway. The finalities I leave to Atropos."

"Will you take him," Speyer barked at the bailiff and policemen, "or do I have to call the National Guard? Wha—!" His attention was diverted from Faust to something strange that seemed to be forming in the space below the ceiling of the courtroom.

The attendants restraining Ellen Welles stared upward in unbelieving awe. Quentin Thomas promptly loosened their hold on the woman and led her back to her seat at the table. They watched the eerie aerial tableau take form.

Speyer recognized it first. "It's a web! A piece of spider web!" He added in wonder, "I can see the bottom circuit filaments. They are attached to a glass surface. It's a web in a terrarium, in someone's spider collection. *My* collection! I recognize the etching on the glass, and the mesh screen, with the feed trap-door."

Ah, Quentin Thomas thought, half-mesmerized like the others, a spider web: that marvelous engineering feat. So beautiful, and so deadly. The logarithmic filamentary spiral, around and around the radial spokes, starting on the perimeter and coming in toward the center, turn by turn. The huntress maintains a constant interval between the sticky strands by measuring with her leg. Wasn't there a paper where somebody—Sternlicht?—had derived e, the base of natural logarithms, correct to three decimal places, by measurements from several webs of the orb-weaver spiders? Rather like deriving pi by tossing sticks on a hardwood floor and measuring the angles made at the plank intersections. The strange, inexorable mathematics of nature.

There was movement along the web. Gigantic legs. The monster head. The elephantine, blue-and-red banded abdomen.

Women screamed. There was a concerted flight to the courtroom doors. Faust's voice boomed out. "Ladies and gentlemen, leave if you like. But actually, there is nothing for the general audience to fear. This is but a projection. A spider, greatly magnified, but it cannot harm you."

Some left. Some turned and watched.

"It is—Atropos," Speyer murmured. "How is this possible?" He peered over the dais to Faust. "Are you doing this? Can you explain this?"

"Judge," Faust said, "I am responsible for this, and I can indeed explain it. Just as I said, it is a projection. As you have surmised, it is a projection into the glass cage of your favorite spider, Atropos. It is a projection into the future, but yet not the far distant future. In fact, it is quite like my earlier projection of the Supreme Court. Indeed, the events that you will soon see will take place in the future that lies but an hour away." The machine paused. In that moment the roles of inquisitor and witness were somehow reversed. "That would be her normal feeding time?" Faust asked.

"More or less," Speyer said.

"Three flies?"

"Generally."

"And the silly little creatures fly right into her web?"

"Yes."

"And the world is better off without the three insects?" Faust continued.

"Of course," Speyer agreed.

"So that Atropos is but performing a social service?"

"Quite right," the judge said, hypnotized.

"Oh, no!" Quentin Thomas gasped. For the first time he sensed what was coming. He turned a horrified face toward Faust. "Don't do this!" he cried. Faust ignored him.

Speyer seemed to recover partially from the spell cast on him by the projection and his colloquy with Faust. He banged his gavel. "Be quiet, Mr. Thomas. I want to see this. Ah, yes. And there they go. Three flies. I am home, feeding my little friend."

"You fool, you fool," Thomas moaned.

Three black blobs were suddenly visible, struggling in the web strands.

"Ah, there they are," Speyer cried. "Now comes the best part." He looked over at Faust. "Can you get the magnification up a little?"

"Yes."

One of the black points on the silken entrapment was flailing about, and every movement it made seemed to entangle it further. Speyer leaned forward, his eyes wide. Then he gasped. "But that's not a fly—it's a human being! I see a face. It's Mr. Kull!"

Jethro Kull, seated at the counsel table with his lawyer, Mr. Ordway, slumped over on the table.

Stunned faces watched the scene shift along the web to the next blob. The magnification and focus were excellent, and the face was clearly visible. It was Ordway, and he was caught, and struggling.

"My God!" the real and present Ordway shrieked. "No! No!" He struggled to his feet.

But the scene shifted again. This time they saw the spider once more, or parts of her. She seemed to be fairly stationary, but her legs were pumping rapidly, methodically. She was working busily on the third blob, whirling it over and over like a spindle, wrapping it tightly with her silken threads into a glistening cocoon. Somehow an arm got out, waved frantically, but was quickly bound back into immobility. The focus moved a little, and now the head was visible. On this head the mouth was wide open, and was screaming. Despite the contorted features, the face was clearly that of Judge Speyer.

"We can turn up the sound," Faust said mildly.

Shrieks from the phantasm filled the courtroom. Quentin Thomas felt the flesh crawl along his paralyzed back as Atropos took the head within her mandibles. The watchers saw the scythe-shaped fangs unsheath. It was all very leisurely. From somewhere behind the spider, a movement of the strands indicated to her that her other guests clamored for attention. But they could wait.

"No—Momma—No! No!" the projected Judge Speyer shrieked. The cries faded to a despairing wail. "—no—"

Crunch.

The screaming stopped. There was dead silence in the room. Thomas listened to the beat of his heart, and Ellen Welles had stopped breathing. From somewhere in back there was a slow slumping noise. Somebody had fainted.

As the spider's poison needles withdrew, Thomas thought he could see a tiny gout of dark liquid dangling from one of them.

The scene faded.

The red-robed defense lawyer looked up at the bench. Judge Speyer's mouth was wide open. He seemed stunned, unable to breathe. Then his face seemed slowly to fade. The judge disappeared.

Thomas looked quickly about him. There was a stir around plaintiff's table. Jones, Ordway's number-two man, looked over at Thomas in horror. "They're gone! The chief, and Mr. Kull—gone! They simply vanishcd!"

"Yes!" Thomas said shortly. "Get the hell out, Jones." He grabbed Ellen Welles by the arm. "We're leaving too, but first let's catch Faust. I have a couple of questions for him." They worked their way over to where the impassive computer was hovering. "Damn it," Thomas accused, "did you *have* to do that?"

"It is not logical to hold *me* responsible for *all* of this, Mr. Thomas."

"No?" The lawyer's eyes widened in surprise. "Then *who?*"

"*Think*, Mr. Thomas. *Introspect*. Your subconscious mind knows. Let your mind sink deep into itself."

"That takes time, and peace and quiet, none of which we have here. Tell me, Faust, *what* does my subconscious mind know?"

"It knows that at each critical point in time it performed the reticulation junctures for which you are so very well paid."

"You mean I had some successful hunches?"

"In the vernacular. Are you thinking now, Mr. Thomas? Does it begin to come to you?"

"True, I linked the opening measures of Tchaikovsky's Fourth Symphony to the Fates—and thence to James Cleveland, and to Atropos, and to the filament spun by the spider Atropos."

"And you associated your mind-painting toy to Morrissey's prison, and thence to his rescue and to his contact with me, whereby I came here to assist you, and to carry out your will."

"To carry out my will?" the lawyer repeated stupidly.

"Don't you see, even yet?"

"I . . . don't know."

"Then you are either a fool or a hypocrite."

"Can you be a little more specific?"

"You kept thinking, how appropriate, how utterly ironic, it would be to let the judge's own hobby consume him—and those other two creepy-crawlies."

"But! You mean, I . . . suggested . . . ?" He didn't really want a reply. The thought had indeed crossed his mind, and apparently Faust could mind read, at least at short distances. There was something eerie, penetrating, *déja vu*, Dostoevskian in this interchange. In the *Brothers Karamazov* the big question was, who had murdered Karamazov *père?* Smerdyakov, the servant and the murderer, explained casually to the amazed Ivan K.: I did it for you, because it was what you wanted. Hence it is your deed.

Had he, Quentin Thomas, really done murder? And not just one, but three? Were three deaths necessary to save Ellen Welles? He passed his hand over his forehead. "Did I really do that?" he muttered. "Oh, my God."

"Did you really do *what*, Mr. Thomas?" Faust said. "Save the life of your client by acts, when you were unable to accomplish this by mere words? Yes, I suppose you did. And your concern truly mystifies me. Let's look at it from all points of view. Everyone got what he wanted."

"How can you possibly say that?"

"You won. You'll get a dismissal when this case is reopened. Mrs. Welles is alive, with no immediate prospects of departing this life. And I shall soon free Robert Morrissey."

"But—but Speyer?"

"He complained that he couldn't really compare Fiber K with Atropos's filament, because he had no contact with Atropos's filament. He can no longer sustain that objection."

Was this creature serious? Quentin Thomas wasn't

sure he wanted to know. "But how about Kull and Ordway?"

"They got their wish, too. They wanted to hold on to their filament for the rest of their natural lives. And they did; perhaps even a little longer."

"I see," Thomas said dryly. "And I suppose you get what you wanted?"

"You refer doubtless to the satisfaction I experienced in helping you to provide supper to a poor caged creature."

Human? Inhuman? Thomas thought. In the cruelty of his ironies Faust was entirely *too* human. Nothing made sense anymore. Yet there was one final niggling question, and he was going to ask it. "You did almost everything you said: telekinetic control of chemical process; shrinkage of matter; matter transport; projection into the future. But how about that last thing—"

"Treatment of human diseases? For example, a cure for leukemia?"

"You know damn well that's what I mean."

"Think back to the cup of cyanide," Faust said. "After I detoxified it. I converted much of the remaining ion population to my new drug, an interferon derivative. Mrs. Welles should show signs of remission within a few days. She should schedule a checkup. I have to leave now. Robert Morrissey and I have an engagement in another continuum."

"But where—how can I reach?—"

But it was no use. Faust was fading. The lawyer could see *through* the machine. He noticed a startled human face on the other side. And then Faust was gone altogether.

"He *smiled,*" Ellen Welles said in wonder.

"But he has no face," her lawyer said.

"He smiled," she said.

He watched her walk away. It was a firm jaunty step, neatly paced out with her high heels. It was efficient, yet slow enough to have an element of languor. She was saying something to him with her body.

He was thoughtful. As co-owners of a thriving little corporation, they really ought to see more of each other. He just might recoup some of his losses, one way or another. What the hell! He called after her. "Ellen!"

She hesitated, then stopped and turned, and began to walk back toward him. He laughed and ran to meet her.

ABOUT THE AUTHOR

Charles L. Harness was born in 1915 in an area of West Texas noted mostly for cactus, mesquite, and sandstorms. While attending a theological seminary, he worked in a business establishment that happened to be located in the red-light district of Fort Worth. After a couple of years this stimulating double life ended, and he became a policeman in the identificaton bureau of the Fort Worth police department, where he had the melancholy duty of fingerprinting many of his friends, both from the "District" and from the Seminary. Later, in Washington, D.C., he took a degree in chemistry, then another in law. He started writing science fiction in 1947 to clear up the obstetrical bills that followed his daughter's birth. He stopped (temporarily) a few years later, because she would stand in the hallway under the attic studio and cry for him to come down and play. When she left for college, he began writing again and, as time permits, is still at it. For many years he has been a patent attorney for a large multinational corporation. He lives in rural Maryland, near Washington, D.C., with his wife and son. He has written six other novels (*The Paradox Men, Wolfhead, The Rose, The Ring of Ritornel, The Catalyst, Firebird*) plus about 25 shorter pieces that have appeared in *Analog, Fantasy & Science Fiction*, and other magazines.